SPORE

Trapped!

Hodge strode past the statue toward the sealed door behind it. Tash noticed he had brought a long metal bar with him. It looked like a cross between an ax and a pry bar.

With an expert thrust he jammed it into the door frame.

"No!" Fandomar suddenly shouted. "Stop!"

Hodge ignored her and pried at the door. The seal looked very old, but it held firm. He leaned his weight into his next push. A tiny crack appeared in the seal.

At that moment, Tash heard a tremendous *BOOM!* from behind them, and the solid rock beneath their feet shook as though a groundquake had begun. A cloud of dust shot up from the ground and hung in the air like a curtain.

When the dust cleared, they could see that an enormous block of stone had dropped from the ceiling of the tunnel and crashed to the floor, closing off the tunnel behind them.

They were trapped inside the asteroid.

Look for a preview of Star Wars: Galaxy of Fear #10, *The Doomsday Ship,* in the back of this book!

STAR WARS®

GALAXY of FEAR

BOOK 9

SPORE

JOHN WHITMAN

BANTAM BOOKS

NEW YORK · TORONTO · LONDON · SYDNEY · AUCKLAND

To Danny, for all his friendship.

RL 6.0, 008–012

SPORE

A Bantam Skylark Book / April 1998

Skylark Books is a registered trademark of Bantam Books, a division of Bantam Doubleday Dell Publishing Group, Inc. Registered in U.S. Patent and Trademark Office and elsewhere.

ISBN 0-553-48639-X

Published simultaneously in the United States and Canada.

Bantam Books are published by Bantam Books, a division of Bantam Doubleday Dell Publishing Group, Inc. Its trademark, consisting of the words "Bantam Books" and the portrayal of a rooster, is Registered in U.S. Patent and Trademark Office and in other countries. Marca Registrada. Bantam Books, 1540 Broadway, New York, New York 10036.

PRINTED IN THE UNITED STATES OF AMERICA
OPM 0 9 8 7 6 5 4 3 2 1

PROLOGUE

In a dark place, it waited.

It had been waiting for hundreds of years.

It couldn't move. Not yet. But soon it would be free.

It could sense living, breathing creatures on the other side of its prison. There had not been living, breathing creatures near it for a very long time. But now they were close.

The thing in the prison could almost smell them. Taste them.

More than anything, it wanted to make contact with them. *Come to me*, it thought. *I want to join you. To join all of you. To know you.*

That was the truth. It wanted to know everyone and everything, to join every living creature.

It sensed that what it wanted was moving closer.

Soon it would be free!

But suddenly the creatures moved away. They left without opening its tomb, without coming close enough for the imprisoned thing to join them.

A feeling of disappointment passed through the thing in the prison. But the feeling did not last long. The thing's home, its tomb, had been discovered. Eventually, someone would open the door. It was patient.

It could wait.

CHAPTER

HELLO.

ANYBODY OUT THERE?

ANYBODY AT ALL?

Thirteen-year-old Tash Arranda leaned back and stared at the words on her computer screen. She had been using the galaxy-wide communications network called the HoloNet. Most people used it to do research. Tash used it to chat with anyone else who was as bored and lonely as she was.

But no one answered.

Turning away from her computer, Tash looked for something else to do. She kept her cabin neat and usually put things away, so there wasn't much in sight. But her eyes did find an object she hadn't put away.

It was a red ball, about the size of her own head,

made of a soft, flexible material. It was a little heavier than it looked, because there were a small computer and an engine built inside.

It was called a speed globe, and it was one of the few objects Tash treasured.

Speed globe was once Tash's favorite game. In speed globe, two teams competed with each other, trying to chase down the fast-moving, computerized globe, which was programmed to avoid everyone. Once one team had caught it, they had to form a chain, handing the globe from one person to another, until they finally bounced it into the goal. The other team would try to stop them. Tash wasn't the greatest athlete, so she was never the best player. But playing speed globe had been fun. She liked being with her friends, and being part of a team.

Sighing, Tash looked away. She didn't play speed globe anymore. Remembering her old friends was just too painful.

Tash clicked off her computer. She didn't feel like talking to anyone, anyway. If that was all she wanted, she could step outside her cabin door. Her twelve-year-old brother, Zak, and their uncle Hoole were both with her on board their ship, the *Shroud*. The trouble was that Zak would jabber about the latest servo motor he had built, and Uncle Hoole would discuss the populations of planets she'd never heard of. They never wanted to talk about the things she wanted to talk about.

Besides, Tash didn't just want company. She wanted

4

to be part of a team, like when she'd played speed globe. She wanted to be with friends her own age. She wanted to feel connected to something.

Of course, it was tough to find another thirteen-year-old girl who'd lost her parents and her friends when her homeworld of Alderaan blew up, been adopted by a Shi'ido uncle who was a shape-shifter, and then learned that she was sensitive to the power the old Jedi Knights called the Force.

She scowled at her reflection in the dark computer screen.

"No moping," she said to herself. "Jedi Knights do not mope."

Of course, she wasn't even close to being a Jedi Knight. That took years of training, and there weren't any Jedi left to teach her. They'd all been killed by the Empire. Just the way her parents and friends had been killed.

There was one person she thought might understand her feelings—a Rebel named Luke Skywalker. She'd met him twice, and she'd had the feeling that he understood the Force, too. But she had no way to contact him. Knowing that Luke was out there somewhere, but unreachable, made the cloud over Tash's head grow darker.

"Aren't you cheerful today," she told her reflection sarcastically. "You need something to shake you out of this gloomy mood."

Suddenly, a voice roared behind her: "Watch out for the hammerhead!"

She jumped up and spun around, just as something slammed at full speed right into her stomach. She cried out in surprise and hit the deck in a pile of arms and legs.

When she sat up, rubbing her stomach, she found Zak beside her, rubbing his head. "You okay?" he asked.

"I think so," Tash replied. "You?"

"I'm prime," Zak said, grinning. "Your stomach isn't nearly as hard as the wall I ran into on the way here."

"What in space are you doing?" she asked as they got to their feet.

Zak shrugged. "Uncle Hoole said we had to stop for supplies, and the closest planet is Ithor. He mentioned that the Ithorians are also called Hammerheads . . ."

". . . so you decided to ram everything on the ship," Tash concluded. "Sometimes I can't believe you and I are related."

Zak pretended to be offended. "It beats boredom."

And loneliness, Tash thought. "I take it back. We're related after all." She added, "Besides, Ithorians are about the last species that would go around ramming people in the stomach."

Zak blinked. "Then why do they call them Hammerheads?"

"You will see momentarily," said the stony voice of Hoole.

The tall Shi'ido seemed to materialize out of nowhere. Their uncle moved so quietly that he often surprised them. In his long robes, he seemed to float across the floor.

Hoole probably could *float across the floor if he wanted to,* Tash thought.

"Are we going planetside?" Zak asked.

"We have already landed," Hoole responded. "I believe you were too busy harassing your sister to notice our descent."

Tash and Zak nearly bolted for the hatch that led outside. They lived aboard the *Shroud,* and any chance to get off the ship was welcome. But Tash's common sense caught up with her at the door, and she turned back to her uncle. "Is it safe?"

"You mean, is there a chance the Imperials might be here to arrest us?" Hoole replied. "It is unlikely. The Ithorians obey Imperial rules like everyone else, but they are not loyal to the Emperor. We should be safe here as long as we do not attract too much attention."

"Gotcha," Zak said as the hatch opened. "We'll just blend right in."

"You think so, huh?" Tash grinned.

"Sure!" Zak stepped out of the ship and his jaw dropped. "Um . . . or not."

An Ithorian waited to greet them. Tash was almost as startled as Zak. She'd seen pictures of Ithorians, but this one's unusual appearance still surprised her.

The Ithorian was just under two meters tall and had two arms and two legs, but that was about as far as the resemblance to humans went. Its bare feet were splayed out and its legs looked like thin tree trunks. And on each hand the Ithorian had three long, delicate fingers and one thumb.

But it was the Ithorian's head that was the most different. Jutting from its thick shoulders was a long, curved neck. Its head was a wide, flat bar and did, indeed, look just like a hammer.

The Ithorian had one eye on each side of its head. Those eyes blinked slowly at Tash and Zak. "Wwell-ccoomme."

Now Tash's jaw dropped. The Ithorian had two mouths, one on each side of its head. Both mouths spoke at once, giving the creature an unbelievably deep, powerful voice. The sound was unusual, but after a moment, Tash's ears adjusted to it.

"Welcome to the *Tafanda Bay*," the Ithorian said.

"Many thanks," Hoole replied, stepping forward. "I am Hoole. This is Tash and Zak Arranda."

The Ithorian nodded solemnly. "I am Fandomar." The Ithorian said the name so delicately that Tash guessed it was female despite the low-pitched voice. "What brings you to Ithor?"

8

Hoole gave few details about himself or the Ar-randas. He was a private person by nature, but since they had been wanted by the Empire he'd become hypercautious. To Fandomar he said only that he was an anthropologist traveling with two young students.

"We need supplies," Hoole added. "May we find them here?"

Fandomar nodded. "The herd ship should have everything you need."

Herd ship? Tash wondered. *A ship for a herd of what?*

But as she stepped away from the *Shroud,* Tash realized what Fandomar meant. She thought they'd landed on a planet. Instead, they had landed inside a gigantic floating city.

Their ship was in a small docking bay covered by a transparent dome. The dome reminded her of the Hologram Fun World, but the Fun World's dome was much smaller. The space dock had been built on a higher level, and Tash could look down and see the rest of the floating city spread out below. Dozens of other domes sprouted around them, connected by bridges and walkways. All the domes rested on a giant floating platform that was dozens of kilometers long.

Rushing to the edge of the dome, Tash looked down. Half a kilometer below the city was a forest-covered planet. She could see waterfalls, lakes, and tree-covered mountains.

"It's beautiful," she said. "Why does everyone live up here? If I were Ithorian, I'd live right in the middle of those forests."

Fandomar replied, "No Ithorian would ever set foot on the surface."

"Really?" Tash asked skeptically, for just then she thought she saw three or four figures scurry out of sight on the ground below the hovering city. "Then who was that?"

Fandomar peered down. A deep, musical noise sounded from her twin mouths. Then she said, "All Ithorians love the forests. That is why we live in these floating cities, which we call herd ships. Living up here, we can make sure that no harm is done to the planet. But for some Ithorians, the connection to the planet is too strong. The Mother Forest calls to them and they go back. They live very simple lives, the way our ancestors did. They have no technology, no machines, and no contact with the herd ships. Officially, what they do is against the law, but we all understand how hard it is to resist the call of the Mother Forest, so they are not punished."

Fandomar showed Hoole and the Arrandas to their quarters on the herd ship. The Ithorians were generous beings who gave free lodging to any visitors who needed to stay overnight.

Zak and Tash stepped into their room. It was small

and cozy, with two cots, two chairs, and a table. Almost every other surface in the room was covered in plants. Plants growing in troughs. Plants growing in buckets. Plants sprouting from containers near windows.

Next to each plant was a small computer display. When touched, the screen described the plant, and a computer voice gave information about Ithor.

Tash studied one display, but Zak ignored the computer and bent down to examine a curious-looking plant on the table. It had broad leaves that were green at the edges but bright orange and yellow in the center, as if they were on fire.

As Zak reached out to touch one of the leaves, the plant suddenly flicked forward and jabbed his hand.

"Ow!" Zak yelped. "That thing just stung me!" He shoved his finger into his mouth.

"Please do not tease the alleth plant." The computer voice explained, "While this sproutling poses no real danger, a full-grown alleth will eat small rodents."

"Now they tell me," Zak grumbled. "I didn't know plants came with instructions." He looked at his sister. "Hey, what's with the speed globe?"

Tash had brought the red globe with her when they left the ship and had been tossing it from hand to hand ever since. She was still feeling a little lonely, and holding the globe reminded her of better times.

"I don't know," she said. "You want to play?"

Zak laughed. "With you? You're terrible!"

11

Tash bristled. She wasn't really mad at Zak, but she was in a bad enough mood to make him eat his words. "In that case, you shouldn't have anything to worry about, Zak. Unless you're afraid I'll win."

Zak laughed. "You're on. But is there anyplace to play here?"

Tash shook her head. "Not *here*. Down there."

She pointed out the window, toward the edge of the transparent dome, and down to the planet's surface.

The generosity of the Ithorians continued to surprise them. Not only had the Hammerheads supplied Hoole, Zak, and Tash with rooms to sleep in, but they had also given them access to small ships called skimmers for traveling around the giant *Tafanda Bay*.

Zak and Tash stood next to one of the small flying ships, but before they could climb in, Zak stopped.

"I'm not sure this is a good idea," he said. "Fandomar said the planet's surface was off limits."

"Don't be such a worry wampa!" Tash replied, tossing the speed globe from one hand to the other.

Zak shook his head. "Since when does my sister break the rules?"

Tash thought a moment. "Well, I'm not breaking the rules exactly. Fandomar said the law wasn't really enforced. Besides, the Ithorians just want to make sure no one harms their planet. We'll be careful."

"I don't know . . . ," Zak said.

12

"Come on, Zak," she pleaded. "It's the perfect time. Uncle Hoole's off resupplying the *Shroud*. He won't be back for a couple of hours."

Zak shook his head. "Okay, but not because I want to see trees. I just want to find out what happens when *you're* the one getting us into trouble."

They climbed into the skimmer and lifted off.

For a while, they cruised around the domes of the *Tafanda Bay*. It looked like any normal city—except that it floated and was nearly covered in the plants that grew in and around the buildings.

Reaching the edge of their dome, Zak and Tash flew through a wide opening and out into the open air. Other ships slipped out before and after them, and most of those ships flew directly toward another dome. As soon as the other ships had passed them, Tash swerved aside and headed for the edge of the floating city. Reaching the edge of the platform, she jerked hard on the skimmer's control stick, sending the ship into a steep dive toward the planet's surface. In moments, they had dropped below the level of the city. As they rushed toward the ground, tall trees seemed to reach up to greet them.

Tash settled the skimmer at the foot of a small hill. A gentle nudge of the engines pushed the skimmer under a large, overhanging rock. Hidden in the shadows, the skimmer wouldn't be spotted by anyone flying overhead. The spot was also far enough from any trees to avoid harming them with the skimmer's exhaust, which made Tash happy. Although she wasn't supposed to be in the forest, she was determined to follow the Ithorians' customs as much as possible.

Popping the hatch, she hopped out of the skimmer with her brother right behind her. She breathed deeply. "Smell that? The air here's so fresh and clean . . ."

She trailed off. The deep breaths she was taking had focused her mind—just like the few times she'd used the Force. Tash suddenly felt something tug at her. Not at her clothes or her hands—at her heart. It was as though there were a string attached to her chest that pulled her toward the forest.

"You okay?" Zak asked.

"Yes," she answered. "Let's play."

Speed globe *was* a team sport, but Zak and Tash did their best. They found an open meadow covered in short green grass, and Tash flicked a switch on the globe. It hummed to life, trembling in her hands. She flicked another switch and the globe shot out of her hands, bouncing to a stop a few meters away.

"Go!" Zak shouted, and dove for the ball. He was fast, but the ball was faster. Just before he could grab it, the speed globe jumped out of the way, powered by its internal engine.

"Nice try," Tash yelled, jumping past her brother. "It's mine!"

But the speed globe dodged away from her, too.

Laughing, Tash and Zak raced across the meadow after the globe. Catching it was nearly impossible—they needed teammates to help corner the globe and grab hold of it. They might never have touched the globe again if it hadn't bounced against a tall tree, coming to a stop in its thick roots.

Tash started forward.

"Hold on," her brother said, tromping up behind her. "What if it's dangerous?"

Tash looked around. Nothing was moving except some of the vines on the tree, stirred by the wind. "What if *what's* dangerous?"

Zak held up his finger. "The tree. Remember that alleth plant that stung me? What if its parents live here?"

"They won't bother you," Tash said, grinning. "Unless you consider yourself a small rodent." She looked around. "It's so peaceful, I'm sure there's nothing dangerous here."

The sentence had barely left her mouth when a bunch of vines wrapped themselves around Zak and pulled him into the air.

CHAPTER

It happened so fast, Tash thought she was seeing things.

One moment, Zak was standing next to her.

The next, he was up in the branches of a nearby tree. For the first few seconds, Tash's brain couldn't figure out how it had happened—she thought her brother had somehow jumped up into the tree, and all she could do was wonder why he was thrashing around up there.

Then Zak managed a strangled cry of "Help!" and she knew he was in trouble.

The vines of the tree were moving. Sharp, jagged leaves protruded from the vines like claws. Several of the vines had already wrapped themselves around Zak's waist, and more were now encircling his neck and throat. When he tried to pry the vines away, tree branches whipped against his arms. "Hel—!" Zak started to yell again before a vine covered his mouth.

"Zak!" Tash shouted. She ran toward the tree.

Which was just what the tree wanted. The moment she stepped within range, a vine stabbed out to loop around her ankle. But the Force was with her. She moved as the vine moved and jumped back just in time.

The tree pulled Zak in even farther, and he nearly disappeared beneath the vines. But Tash could still see his feet kicking, and the thrashing vines told her that her brother was putting up a good fight.

Again and again Tash tried to rush forward, but each time the tree was waiting for her. Tash picked up a rock and threw it at the tree. The stone bounced off the tree's hard trunk—nothing happened. But she had no other weapon to use. In frustration, she picked up a larger rock.

"That won't help," said a deep, calm voice.

Tash nearly dropped the rock on her foot.

Standing behind her, gazing with kind, friendly eyes, was Fandomar the Ithorian.

"Help!" Tash insisted. "It'll kill him."

Without answering, Fandomar stepped past Tash and walked right into the shade of the thrashing tree. Over the hissing sound of scraping leaves, Tash heard

Fandomar talk to the tree in a soft, throaty whisper. Tash couldn't understand the words, but the voice was so soothing that she felt instantly calm.

Fandomar's voice had the same effect on the tree. Its moving limbs became still. A thick bunch of vines suddenly unrolled toward the ground, revealing Zak, who had been wrapped up as tightly as a mummy from Necropolis. His face was a deep shade of red and his eyes looked as if they'd almost been squeezed out of his head.

Still frightened of the tree, Tash kept an eye on its branches as she ran to her brother's side. She caught him just as his knees gave out.

"Are you hurt?" she asked.

Zak shook his head. "I'm okay." Then, with a gasp, he added, "Breathing—it's a very good thing."

"He should recover shortly," Fandomar said.

Tash moved quickly out of the shade of the predatory tree. "Your planet looks so peaceful," she said to the Ithorian. "I can't believe you have such dangerous trees. You should cut them down."

Fandomar stiffened, and Tash realized she had offended the Ithorian, who said, "We obey the Law of Life. We do not harm living things."

"But that tree almost killed Zak," Tash said, a little more gently.

Patiently, Fandomar opened her delicate fingers in a

gesture like a human shrug. "The vesuvague is not dangerous. At least not to Ithorians."

"Vesu—?" Tash tried to repeat.

"Veh-soo-vog," Fandomar repeated slowly, pronouncing the word for her.

Zak coughed. When he felt that he could talk normally, he said, "Thanks, Fandomar. If you hadn't come by, I would have been plant food."

"What did you say to the tree?" Tash asked Fandomar.

The Ithorian replied, "It's not what I said, but how I said it. Ithorians—especially the High Priests—are very connected to the Mother Forest. They know how to speak to the trees."

"Then you're a High Priest?" Tash asked.

Fandomar waved her fingers again. *It* is *a shrug,* Tash thought. *It's what she does when she doesn't want to say anything.*

Fandomar walked them back to their skimmer. To Tash's surprise, she had landed her own little ship under the same overhang. Had Fandomar seen them land? Or was she just trying to hide her ship, too?

"I know we're not supposed to be down here," Tash quickly told Fandomar. "I'm sorry. We—I mean, I— just wanted to see the forest. We didn't realize—"

"I understand," Fandomar interrupted. "No harm has been done."

Tash thanked the stars that Ithorians were so understanding. She'd met plenty of species who would have screamed at them for disobeying local customs. She decided to push her luck.

"Um, there's one more thing. Do you think—I mean, would you mind not telling our uncle about this? As long as no harm was done."

The Ithorian nodded. "I agree. As long as you promise not to tell anyone that you saw me down here."

So Fandomar *had* wanted to hide her ship. "You aren't a High Priest, are you?" Tash guessed. "You're not supposed to be down here, either."

Fandomar nodded. "That is correct. I think it's in both our interests to keep this secret to ourselves."

"Secrets," Zak groaned. On a recent visit to the planet S'krrr, he'd kept a secret that nearly cost them all their lives. "I swore I'd never keep a secret like this again."

"To seal our agreement," Fandomar said, "let me show you something few offworlders have ever seen."

They were standing at the edge of an enormous grove of trees with shining black bark. They weren't vesuvague trees. This was like a forest within the forest—a wood so thick and deep that Tash could hardly see beyond the first few branches.

"This is the oldest grove of Bafforr trees on Ithor," Fandomar explained. "Bafforr trees are sentient."

"Sentient?" Zak repeated.

"That means they can think. They're intelligent," Tash explained.

Fandomar nodded. "The more trees there are, the more intelligent the forest becomes. It's as though one mind connects them all so that they can all work together."

"Work together," Tash repeated. "Like a team. That's what I want." More loudly, she asked, "Can we *talk* to them?"

Fandomar shook her head. "High Priests can. They are very sensitive to the Bafforrs' thoughts. But without that sensitivity, you cannot hear them."

Tash said, "It sounds like you're talking about the Force."

Fandomar's two mouths turned down. "No. The High Priests aren't Jedi Knights. Their sensitivity is different."

Tash wondered if she could reach the trees anyway. She'd only learned a little bit about the Force, but according to what she had read, the Force connected all living things. If that was true, why couldn't it connect her to the Bafforr trees?

Focusing her thoughts, she reached out with the Force. She took a deep breath to clear her head and then felt it—like an invisible hand stretching toward the forest. For just a brief instant, she felt something reach back in response. An excited tingle ran through her arms. The Bafforr trees were aware of her!

For that moment, she felt a powerful connection with the trees. She couldn't have described it if she tried. It was like . . . It was like playing speed globe with a really good team, with everyone working together. Only it was a thousand times more satisfying than just playing a game.

Excited, Tash pushed harder. She wanted to be a Jedi Knight. She *needed* to be one, but she had no way of testing herself. If she could communicate with the Bafforr trees, that might mean the Force was still with her, that her power was growing.

But she tried too hard. The more she thought about trying to use the Force, the harder it became to use it, until finally, it just slipped away.

"What's wrong, Tash?" Zak asked.

She sighed. Zak wouldn't understand. "Nothing. Come on, let's go."

She turned away from the forest, feeling lonelier than ever.

Fandomar followed them back up to the *Tafanda Bay* and walked them to their quarters. Uncle Hoole had returned from his errands.

He studied his niece and nephew for a moment, as

though he were bracing himself for bad news. When none came, his gray face twisted into a look of amusement. "This is a pleasure," he said. "I have left you alone for several hours, and nothing eventful has happened. No Imperial invasions. No dangerous criminals."

"We haven't uncovered one evil plot," Tash agreed, casually tossing her speed globe from hand to hand. "Did you get everything we need?"

Hoole frowned. "Unfortunately not. The Ithorians do not do much mining. I need a supply of the mineral ethromite."

"What's ethromite?" Tash asked.

Zak answered, "It's one of the minerals used to create the fusion reactions that power starship engines."

"And it seems to be in scarce supply here," Hoole added.

Fandomar raised one long finger to get their attention. "I believe I can help."

Not only did Fandomar know where they could acquire more ethromite, but she also offered to take Hoole and the two Arrandas there. Not far from the planet Ithor was a large asteroid field where a group of humans had set up a mining colony. Fandomar's job aboard the *Tafanda Bay* was to pilot a shuttle that ferried supplies to and from the mining colony. Although she was not scheduled to return to the colony for several days, she would be happy to take Hoole and the Arrandas out on a special mission.

A short time later, they climbed aboard an old but well-kept cargo ship and streaked out of the planet's atmosphere. Through the viewport Tash watched the stars rush toward the ship.

A short journey took them into a wide band of rocks whirling through space—asteroids. Some of the asteroids were as small as Tash's head; others seemed as big as moons. Some drifted by slowly while others flashed by as fast as comets. Tash had still been holding the speed globe, but now she dropped it and gripped the edge of her seat until her knuckles turned white. One wrong turn in an asteroid field would convert them into an exploding fireball.

"This is dangerous work," Hoole stated.

Fandomar nodded, concentrating on the deadly rocks spinning past the ship. Tash closed her eyes.

"It seems like you get stuck with all the jobs no one else wants," Zak noted. "Greeting people at the space dock, piloting shuttles. Don't you want to be doing something more important?"

Hoole winced at Zak's impoliteness, but Fandomar only nodded. "I am . . . doing penance."

"Penance?" Tash asked, opening one eye. "You mean you're being punished?"

"In a sense," the Ithorian explained. "Only . . . I

have *chosen* these tasks. I have volunteered to make this run."

"Why?" Hoole asked. "I thought Ithorians preferred not to travel too far from the Mother Forest and their herd ships."

"True," Fandomar replied. "But my husband was exiled from Ithor several years ago. Although he would not let me go with him, I swore to myself that I would not sit comfortably aboard the *Tafanda Bay* until his return."

"What did he do?" Zak asked.

Fandomar opened her twin mouths to reply. But instead, she suddenly jerked the controls hard to one side, throwing the ship into a confused spin.

For a moment Tash thought the Ithorian had gone crazy.

Until she saw the sharp teeth of the giant worm that was lunging to swallow their ship!

CHAPTER 3

"Space slug!" Hoole warned.

Tash's eyes went wide with fear. She had never seen a space slug before. The slug had sprung from a cave in a nearby asteroid. The hole in the flying rock was large enough to let a starship through, and the slug filled every meter. Tash caught a glimpse of the thick, gray body slithering out of its cave, and its huge eyeless head. But then the slug's body, the asteroids, even the stars around them, vanished as the space slug opened its huge jaws to swallow them.

Fandomar jerked on the controls again and the cargo ship lurched in the other direction. Tash's crashwebbing snapped and she went flying, slamming her shoulder against the side of the ship.

Fandomar's move saved their lives. Instead of

chomping on them, the space slug only tapped their ship with the side of its massive head. Their shields held, but the ship spun wildly out of control.

"We've got to get out of here," Hoole grunted. "Out of its range."

"No good," Fandomar replied. "The engines aren't responding."

Tash pointed to the asteroids rocketing through space around them. "We're drifting! One of those asteroids will hit us!"

"Not if the space slug gets us first!" Zak yelled.

They were still in the huge slug's range. Its head and part of its body twisted wildly from the cave, trying to reach them. The slug turned its head toward them and opened its mouth again to strike.

"Move the ship!" Tash yelled.

"I cannot!" Fandomar shouted back.

The space slug stabbed at them again.

But before it could reach them, the slug recoiled in pain as a streak of light punctured its skin.

Laser beams!

Someone was firing blaster bolts at the space slug.

The slug hesitated. It seemed to be attracted by the rapid movements and flashing lights of three tiny yellow ships that crisscrossed and zigzagged around it. The ships were hardly bigger than a human being and they moved with incredible speed, flying circles around the giant slug. Laser beams flashed from the ships and penetrated the slug's skin like needles. As the three ships continued to pour fire onto the slug, the creature shut its mouth and coiled back into its hole.

"Cargo ship, this is *Starfly One*," said a welcoming voice over Fandomar's comm. "Looks like you could use a little help."

The three small craft formed a triangle around Fandomar's damaged cargo cruiser and locked onto it with tractor beams. One Starfly pulled them and the others pushed the cargo ship forward with their beams. Once they had the larger ship under control, they headed back toward the asteroid field.

"We're not going back there, are we?" Tash gasped as a huge asteroid flew by.

"Have no fear," Fandomar explained calmly. "The Starflies are specifically designed for flight through the asteroids. They're small and maneuverable enough to get around the rocks. Their tractor beams can push as well as pull. The miners use them to move space rocks out of their paths, but they'll work just as well at moving us. These miners know how to handle asteroids."

She was right. The pilots seemed to have a sixth sense for where the space rocks would move. Even hauling the damaged cargo ship, they slipped easily through the gaps in the swarm of asteroids.

In a few moments, the Starflies dropped toward an asteroid that was almost the size of a planet. Tash saw a small collection of buildings clinging to its rocky surface. The Starflies hauled their passengers into a docking bay. Tash, Zak, and Hoole waited until the docking-bay door had closed and oxygen had flooded into the chamber.

They hopped out of their ship and hurried to the nearest Starfly.

"Look how small these ships are!" Zak said appreciatively. "They're hardly bigger than a landspeeder. I can't believe they have enough room for life-support systems."

"They do not," Fandomar answered. "The pilots must wear spacesuits while flying."

Just then the Starfly's hatch broke open and a large human in a flight suit and helmet jumped out. He gave a few orders to his two companions, who hurried from the docking bay. As the big man removed his helmet, Tash saw short-cropped gray hair and a friendly smile. The man shook their hands and said, "Welcome to Mining Station Alpha. I'm the chief miner, but we're a small outfit here, only me and the other two, so just call me Hodge."

Hoole bowed slightly. "We owe you our thanks. That slug would have swallowed us in moments."

Hodge nodded. "The asteroid field's infested with them. I knew one of those giant worms would get Fandomar one of these days."

"I was distracted," the Ithorian admitted, coming up behind.

"So!" Hodge clapped his hands together eagerly. "We don't get many visitors out here. What can we do for you?"

Hoole told Hodge the same story he'd told Fandomar, giving few details. "We need ethromite to power our ship."

Hodge nodded. "We got plenty of that. It may cost you, though."

Hoole nodded. "I am sure I have enough credits—"

Hodge waved his hands and grinned. "Nope, don't need credits. We make plenty off the Ithorians here." He chuckled at Fandomar. "I'd rather make a trade. If you're an anthropologist, you may be able to answer a few questions. I'll give you all the ethromite you need if you help us solve a little mystery."

Tash watched Hoole's expression. She could tell he wanted to get the ethromite as quickly as possible, but she also knew he loved to explore different cultures. "Very well. As long as it will put the children in no danger."

"Naw!" the big miner laughed. "No danger. Just a little space walk is all."

An hour later, Tash found herself walking on the surface of the asteroid. She was wearing a bulky spacesuit and a clear round fishbowl of a helmet. On her back she carried an oxygen tank and a small computer—the brains of the suit. The computer maintained a constant temperature inside the suit and pumped oxygen into her helmet.

Tash's heart pounded against her ribs. She craned her neck forward and touched her nose to the plastiform faceplate of her helmet. Only a thin sheet of plastiform protected her from the icy cold vacuum of space. Only a few layers of protective fabric kept her from instant death.

"Look up, Tash," Zak said. She heard his voice through the comlink speaker in her helmet.

Tash looked up and immediately felt dizzy. The asteroid field was just as frightening as before. In fact, it was scarier. Rocks the size of mountains hurtled over their heads. She felt just like one of the space rocks herself—spinning around, hurtling alone through the dark vacuum.

"There's no 'up' in space, laser brain," she told Zak irritably. "And there's no down, either. That's because there isn't any gravity."

Tash stamped her feet slowly. Her thick boots kicked up a cloud of dust that hung over the ground. The boots were specially designed for use on asteroids with zero gravity. The usual gravity boots—the kind used in spaceships—were equipped with magnetic soles so that they would stick to the metal of the ship. But since the ground on an asteroid was nonmagnetic, the miners used boots equipped with mini–tractor beams instead of magnets. The tractor beams pulled her feet toward the ground. On the planet Ithor, she would hardly be able to lift these boots. But in the weightlessness of space, they all had to wear special grav-boots to keep from floating right off the asteroid.

They were marching along the asteroid's surface, with Hodge in the lead. Fandomar followed Hodge in a spacesuit specially designed to fit Ithorians' bodies. Then came Zak and Tash. Hoole brought up the rear.

Hodge led them to the edge of a giant pit. Unlike the rough surface of the asteroid, the sides of the pit were very smooth, as if something had been sliding in and out of it for years.

"A slug hole," Tash guessed.

"Right," Hodge's voice crackled over the comlink. "But the slug's long gone."

"How do we get down there?" Zak asked, peering down into the rocky tunnel.

"Like this," the miner said.

He jumped into the hole.

Without gravity, he might have hung in empty space forever. But his grav-boots pulled him downward, and slowly he began to descend into the slug tunnel. Fandomar followed a moment later.

Zak and Tash looked at Hoole, who gave the slightest nod.

They all jumped.

Tash fell in super slow motion. She had plenty of time for her eyes to adjust to the dark tunnel, and she watched the bottom slowly rise up to meet her. The tunnel wasn't very deep. It dropped straight down for a few dozen meters, then curved sharply to one side and leveled off. She landed at the curve with an easy bounce.

Hodge had lit a bright glowrod and motioned for them to follow him.

The cavern was huge. The slug that had filled the hole must have been a hundred meters thick.

Tash slid her hand along the wall as they continued their hike. It was as smooth as glass. She could hardly believe that any creature lived in deep space. It was amazing that the slugs didn't need air to breathe or sunlight for warmth.

Deep in thought, Tash didn't notice that the walls were closing in. The tunnel was tapering off. She didn't notice that the others had stopped moving until she bumped into something hard and gray standing in front of her. She looked up . . .

. . . into the face of an Ithorian, standing there without a spacesuit, its two mouths twisted into a look of absolute terror.

CHAPTER

Tash let out a warning shout right into her comlink microphone. Everyone around her jumped as the sound of her voice blasted into their helmets.

Zak put his gloved hands on the sides of his helmet as if he were trying to plug his ears. "Tash! Turn down the volume. It's only a—"

A statue. She could see that now. It was a statue of an Ithorian. It was holding both hands up in a warning gesture. In the light of Hodge's glowrod, the statue's face looked both angry and frightened.

"Curious," Hoole muttered. He was talking to himself, but they could all hear him as clearly as they'd heard Tash shout. The Shi'ido stepped past the statue. The tunnel ended just a few meters beyond. Set in the very end of the tunnel was a thick durasteel door.

Hodge pointed up to a hole in the tunnel ceiling. A shaft had been dug down from the surface of the asteroid. The chief miner explained, "We were digging down from the surface, looking for minerals. Our laser drill broke through into this empty space. We knew it had to be a worm tunnel, so we found the tunnel opening and used it to get down here. We found this."

"Fandomar," Hoole said after he'd examined the statue for a moment. "I was not aware that the Ithorians made statues like this. Most Ithorian artwork involves plants and animals. What do you make of this?"

Fandomar raised her hands. "I couldn't say."

Hodge held his glowrod up to the statue's face. "I've been around Ithorians enough to know their expressions. This one looks angry or frightened. Or both."

"It's like a warning," Tash said.

Zak scoffed. "There are a lot better ways to warn people," he said. "How about a holographic message? Warning beacons. Signs."

Hodge answered. "All that kind of stuff was here. At least we think it was."

He pointed to a section of the tunnel wall near the statue. Someone had cut an alcove into the smooth rock. In the alcove they saw the remains of a generator and a few strands of cable. The cable wires had been cut.

"This is how we found it," the chief miner explained. "Me and my boys don't normally go into worm holes. But we got readings on a good supply of

35

minerals down here, so we risked it and found this. That doorway is sealed shut. We didn't know what to make of it.''

"Maybe you should report it to the Ithorians," Tash suggested.

"We did," Hodge said, nodding toward Fandomar.

Fandomar blinked. "My people had no response."

Hoole looked from the statue to the cut wires and back to the statue again. Finally, he said, "I believe the statue *is* a warning. I suspect it is some sort of fail-safe in case the power supply for the true warning device ever failed." Hoole pointed to the base of the statue. A long rectangular section of the stone looked discolored. "It looks like someone removed something from the statue. Probably there was a written warning carved into the stone."

Tash bent down to examine the spot. There had been a sign there. She could see that part of it had broken when the mysterious intruders had snapped it off. Even if Tash could have read the language, only parts of the words were visible.

"So who removed the warning?" Zak asked.

"And who put it here in the first place?" Tash added.

"Ithorians, obviously," Hoole decided. "I would guess that what lies behind that door is a tomb. But the question is: Why would Ithorians, who rarely leave their home planet, fly out to this barren asteroid field to bury someone, or something, in the bottom of a worm tunnel?''

Hodge grunted. ''I was hoping you could help, being an anthropologist and all. I guess there's only one way to find out what it is.''

Hoole shook his head. ''I think we should get the permission of the Ithorians before doing anything here.''

The chief miner replied, ''It's not really their call. Me and my men own this rock now. I've been itching to find out what's behind this door. Whether it's a tomb or not, I figure there must be something important down here for someone to go to so much trouble. Could be worth a lot of money. If you can't tell me, I know another way to find out.''

He strode past the statue toward the sealed door behind it. Tash noticed he had brought a long metal bar with him. It looked like a cross between an ax and a pry bar. With an expert thrust he jammed it into the door frame.

''No!'' Fandomar suddenly shouted. ''Stop!''

Hodge ignored her and pried at the door. The seal looked very old, but it held firm. He leaned his weight into his next push. A tiny crack appeared in the seal.

At that moment, Tash heard a tremendous *BOOM!* from behind them, and the solid rock beneath their feet shook as though a groundquake had begun. A cloud of dust shot up and hung in the air like a curtain.

When the dust cleared, they could see that an enormous block of stone had dropped from the ceiling of the tunnel and crashed to the floor, closing off the way they had entered.

They were trapped inside the asteroid.

CHAPTER

5

The five explorers hurried toward the stone and pushed. It wouldn't budge.

"A trap," Hoole muttered into his comlink. "I should have suspected. This tomb, or whatever it is, was not meant to be opened."

"I gotta agree with you now," Hodge said. "No more messing with the door." He flipped a switch on his comlink. "Alpha Station, this is Hodge." He waited. "Alpha Station, this is Hodge. Do you copy?" The only answer he got was static. He grunted. "The signal's not getting through. The rock's too thick."

"They'll come looking for us, won't they?" Tash asked.

"Yeah," Hodge agreed. He checked the monitor attached to his wrist. "I hope our air holds out long enough."

Tash looked at her own wrist. A small screen display showed how much air she had left in her tank. She had enough oxygen for another twenty minutes. After that, she would suffocate inside her spacesuit.

"Uncle Hoole," she asked, "can't you . . . do something?"

She wanted to say "Can't you shape-shift?" but she knew Hoole liked to keep his powers to himself if possible.

Hoole shook his head and said simply, "No air."

It took Tash a moment to realize what he meant. As far as she knew, her uncle could change into any living creature—even a creature like a Wookiee that was big and strong enough to lift the block of stone. But Wookiees had to breathe, and there was no air outside their spacesuits.

Besides, Tash guessed, *he might not be able to shape-shift while he's inside the suit.*

She glanced from face to face, hoping someone would have a suggestion. When her eyes fell on Fandomar, she realized that the Ithorian had said almost nothing. She was standing off to one side. She looked as if she were ready to stay in the tunnel forever.

"I've got an idea," Hodge said. "But it might be dangerous."

"Don't worry," Zak snorted. "We're getting used to danger."

Hodge's plan was simple. The shaft the miners had dug into the tunnel went straight up to the surface of the asteroid. All they had to do was stand beneath it, deactivate their gravity boots, and float right up to the surface.

"Only problem is," the chief miner ended, "the shaft's too narrow for anyone but the kids."

"No problem," Zak said. "I'm on my way."

Tash hesitated for a moment. She thought she ought to volunteer ahead of her younger brother. But the thought of being alone on the asteroid's surface scared her. She decided to let Zak take the lead.

Hodge, however, disagreed. "Sorry, son, but I think your shoulders are a little too wide." The miner held his hands up to Zak's shoulders. "Yep, you're wider than our laser drill." Hodge kept his hands the same distance apart and measured Tash's shoulders. "But you can make it."

Tash was shocked. Since when was Zak bigger than she was? She stared at her younger brother. She was still taller than he was. But Zak had started to fill out. Tash shook her head. She really was out of touch. She hadn't even noticed her own little brother growing up.

She took a deep breath. "Okay." Hoole stepped between her and Hodge. "Tash—" he started to say; then he stopped. The gray-faced Shi'ido looked around as though he were trying to find another solution. When he couldn't find one, he looked back at Tash. An expression of concern flickered across his face; then he said, "Be careful."

Hodge led Tash to a spot a few meters away from the statue. Looking up, she saw the mineshaft disappear into the darkness. "Remember," she heard Hodge say, "be sure to reactivate your boots the moment you clear the tunnel."

She nodded. Then she reached down and pressed a button on the heel of each shoe.

Immediately, Tash felt herself become weightless. Her feet were still touching the rocky floor, but she didn't feel connected to it anymore.

Taking a deep breath, she jumped upward and began to slowly rise toward the ceiling. Or was the ceiling dropping down to meet her? She couldn't tell.

She touched the tunnel with her gloved hands and guided herself straight into the mineshaft. Her space helmet and shoulders just barely fit into the hole.

It got dark very, very quickly.

"Good job, Tash!" she heard Zak cheer.

"Well done," Hoole's voice added.

She thought she heard someone else speak, but the voice was cut off by static. The thick rock interfered with their short-range comlinks.

She was alone in the dark.

With no sound and no light and the strange feeling that she was hardly even moving, Tash felt really alone.

It must have only been a few minutes, but it felt as if she'd been floating for hours.

Just when she started to panic, her head suddenly cleared the tunnel. She had reached the surface! Starlight glittered on the dusty asteroid. A shower of asteroids rushed by overhead. After the darkness of the tunnel, all the movement made her dizzy and she forgot what she was supposed to do next. She was floating ten meters above the surface before she remembered to reactivate her boots.

The tractor beams kicked in. She felt as if something had grabbed hold of her ankles. She settled gently onto the surface.

Bounding across the zero-gravity terrain, she made a quick trip back to the mining colony. She was so eager to find help, she didn't notice that three additional Starflies had suddenly appeared inside the docking bay. As she entered the air-filled halls of the colony, she pulled off her helmet and shouted, "Help! Somebody help us!"

"Why, whatever can I do for you, my dear?" said a voice as thin and sharp as a razor blade.

As Tash turned toward the voice, a wave of sheer terror overwhelmed her. She recognized the feeling. It was the dark side of the Force. She had felt it only once before, in the presence of Darth Vader! She felt it again now, like an ice-cold blast of air all around her.

It was going to freeze her heart.

CHAPTER

6

The man who had spoken was tall, and thin like a skeleton. He was dressed entirely in black. His head was bald and his skin was dark. Tattoos covered the lower part of his face. Strangest of all, he wore a band of black cloth over both eyes.

If he even has *eyes,* Tash thought. But he had to be able to see. He was staring right at her, and when he took a step closer, he moved easily across the room.

How does he see? she wondered.

Then she felt another wave of dark-side energy crash against her. The man was reaching out with the dark side of the Force, using it the way insects used their antennae to feel their way around.

The tattooed man's dark-side energy wasn't quite as powerful as the feeling she'd gotten from Darth Vader months ago. This man wasn't as strong as Vader. But he was almost as evil.

Behind him, Tash saw the other two miners sitting quietly and nervously. Two stormtroopers stood at attention on either side of them, blasters in hand.

The Empire. If they knew who Tash was, then she, Zak, and Hoole were doomed.

"Who—?" she started to ask.

"Never mind," the man in black replied. "Where are the others?"

Tash told him. The man clenched his jaw. "Have they opened the door?"

"No, sir," she replied. Her mouth was dry.

He relaxed a bit. A slight smile crossed his face, wrinkling the weird tattoos on his jaw. "Then they may yet live."

The members of the exploring party were back in the mining colony, removing their suits just as the last of their oxygen was used up.

The man in black had sent his two stormtroopers with Tash. They had found a mechanism that lifted the block of stone from the outside, and had easily freed the prisoners. The troopers had then marched them back to the mining colony at gunpoint. Now Zak, Tash, Hoole, and Fandomar sat in the main hall of the mining facility with Hodge and the other two miners.

"My name," the man in black began, "is Jerec. I am a servant of His Imperial Majesty, the Emperor."

Tash felt Hoole tense beside her. If Jerec knew who they were, they'd have to fight their way out of the room.

But if Jerec had heard of these three criminals, he wasn't interested. "That tunnel and its contents are now the property of the Empire," he declared. "Entry is forbidden."

"But we own the deed to that mine!" Hodge protested. "It belongs to—"

"You may discuss it," Jerec said in a voice like a vibroblade, "with the Emperor. I can arrange a personal interview."

The way he said "interview" made it sound more like "torture." Hodge said nothing.

Hoole filled the silence. "I feel you should know that, whatever is buried down there, the Ithorians seem sure that it should not be dug up."

"What the Ithorians want is no concern of mine," Jerec snapped.

"But . . . ," Fandomar began. It was the first time she'd spoken in over an hour. "But it could be . . . dangerous."

Jerec turned toward Fandomar. Again, even though his eyes were hidden behind the black band, Tash felt that he was *seeing* something. The presence of the dark side grew stronger. This man definitely knew how to use the Force—for evil.

"You are Fandomar," Jerec stated. "Your husband is Momaw Nadon, the Ithorian in exile."

"Yes," she confessed.

"Then I would be quiet, if I were you," Jerec said threateningly. "Unless you want me to tell your people your husband's last little secret."

Fandomar closed both her mouths.

Jerec turned to Hodge. "You will take me to this tunnel, and there you will tell me everything you know about it. Now."

Hodge hesitated. "I don't think this is a good time."

Jerec snapped his fingers and one of the stormtroopers put a blaster to Hodge's head. "You will take me to this tunnel now, or your friends will wipe your remains off the floor."

Hodge's face turned pale. "Whatever you say. It's just that this is prime hunting time for the space slugs. They'll be more alert than usual, and you never know when a slug's asteroid will pass right overhead. It would be better to wait a few hours until they calm down again."

For a moment, Jerec did not move. Tash felt her skin crawl as waves of dark-side power passed through her again. She knew that Jerec was trying to tell whether Hodge was being honest.

"Very well," Jerec said. He turned to his stormtroopers. "Disable this station's comlink antenna. No one is allowed to send messages from this lifeless rock. Then stand guard over all the ships." He smiled cruelly. "No one is allowed on or off this asteroid until I have examined that tunnel."

"What do you think he wants?" Zak whispered to Tash.

They were sitting in what must have been the mining facility's entertainment room. There was a hologame board, several vidscreens, and shelves full of holodisks. Tash and Zak hadn't touched any of them. Instead, they'd settled in front of a small computer. Tash was riffling through its files.

None of the Imperials were in the room. Jerec had accepted Uncle Hoole's story, which was mostly true anyway, that they'd been on their way to the planet Bespin when they'd stopped at Ithor for supplies. The Imperial had seemed more interested in relaying messages to his Star Destroyer, which was hovering just outside the asteroid field. With his mind focused on other things, Jerec had hardly paid any attention to them at all.

Even though no Imperials were in sight, Tash whispered anyway. "I don't know. He talks like he knows what's behind that door. And he wants it."

"Then it can't be good," her brother said.

"I agree," Hoole said. The Shi'ido had sneaked up on them again, giving Zak and Tash a start.

"Uncle Hoole!" Zak said, clutching his heart. "You know, you're almost as scary as that Jerec."

"Do you know anything about him?" Tash asked. "I mean, is he human? Why does he wear that black band over his eyes?"

"And those tattoos on his face," Zak said. "Are they natural, or did someone put them there?"

Hoole shook his head. "I'm afraid I'm unfamiliar with Jerec. He appears human, but I suspect he is not. My guess is that blindness is natural to his species. However, this is no time to question him about his origin."

Hoole pointed to the screen. "Besides, I came to ask questions, not answer them. I thought I would find you at a computer, Tash. Have you had any luck finding information?"

Tash sighed and admitted, "No. The miners did a lot of research about Ithor when they built this place. The records go back thousands of years. There are records for almost every herd ship, every day, for two thousand years. I can tell you almost anything you would want to know about Ithor. But there's nothing about this asteroid."

"Do you get the feeling Fandomar knows more than she's saying?" Zak asked. "She was awfully quiet while we were trying to figure out how to get out of the tunnel."

Tash nodded. "Yeah, I noticed that, too. But I don't

think she knew about the trap. There's no way she'd do anything to hurt us.''

''Why not?'' Zak asked.

''The Law of Life, remember? Fandomar wouldn't hurt a Circarpousian swamp fly, let alone another sentient being,'' Tash said.

''Maybe she's decided to break the law,'' Zak suggested. ''Her husband's an outlaw, after all.''

Hoole nodded. ''Jerec mentioned Fandomar's husband, Momaw Nadon. She said he was exiled from Ithor. Can you find out what he did?''

Tash nodded. ''Already did. According to the records, the Ithorians know a lot about gene-splicing.''

''Is that like making clones?'' Zak asked.

''Not exactly,'' Hoole replied. ''Clones are exact copies. In gene-splicing, scientists combine the genes of many different life-forms to make a new one.''

Tash continued, ''Apparently the Ithorians kept their knowledge to themselves. Momaw Nadon was a High Priest, so he knew all about that stuff. Some Imperial wanted this secret knowledge and forced Momaw to tell him. Even though Momaw did it to save lives, the Ithorians banished him for revealing their secrets.''

''That is not prime,'' Zak muttered.

''Gene-splicing. Imperials,'' Hoole muttered. He wrinkled his dark brow. He looked as if he were trying to put together the pieces of a puzzle. "Tash, you said there was a record for *almost* every day. Is something missing?"

His niece nodded. "There's a gap in the records. For almost a hundred years, nothing is recorded. Then the records start again without mentioning the missing time."

"Curious," Hoole mused. "Perhaps—"

But he was interrupted by one of the stormtroopers, who stomped into the room and growled, "Time to go."

In the docking bay, under the stormtrooper's watchful eye, Hoole and the two Arrandas slipped into their spacesuits. Jerec, already dressed in a protective suit, waited impatiently.

The other stormtrooper marched into the docking bay with one of the miners and reported, "I could only find this man. Hodge and the other miner are missing."

"Where are they?" Jerec demanded.

"Here I am!" said Hodge. He came trotting into the docking bay already dressed in his flight suit. He smiled, but his eyes flitted nervously from person to person. He seemed to be looking for something.

"Where is your companion?" Jerec demanded.

Hodge hesitated for a fraction of a second. "He went ahead to make sure it was safe."

Tash could tell that Jerec was suspicious. He ordered one of his stormtroopers to remain behind and guard the Starflies to make sure no one left the asteroid. Then he led the way out onto the surface, with the others following. The second stormtrooper brought up the rear. Tash couldn't help noticing that his blaster was set to kill.

They marched along, back toward the slug tunnel. The asteroid was as lifeless as before—except for one change. In the distance, near the tunnel entrance, they could see a small, white figure. As they got nearer, they saw that it was a man in a spacesuit.

"There he is," Hodge said. "I told you he was just making sure it's safe."

They continued toward him. The man did not move. He stood there, waiting for them.

They drew nearer, and still the figure didn't move. He stood perfectly still. Even from a distance, Tash could tell there was something strange about the way he was standing. As they came within a few dozen meters, she realized what it was. He was holding both hands above his head.

He had been holding them above his head the *whole* time.

They reached the mine. The figure still hadn't taken a single step, and his arms were still reaching over his head.

Tash blinked. His arms weren't reaching. They were floating.

Inside his space helmet, the miner's face was frozen in an expression of horror.

Even though he was standing on his feet, the man in the spacesuit was obviously dead.

CHAPTER 7

By the look on the miner's face, whatever had killed him had filled him with surprise and terror.

It reminded her of the look on the face of the Ithorian statue.

"But if he's dead, how is he still . . . standing there?" she whispered.

"Grav-boots," Jerec said. He pointed at the miner's feet. The mini–tractor beams in the victim's gravity boots were still functioning. They had pinned his feet to the surface of the asteroid while the rest of his body tried to float away.

Taking command of the situation, Jerec approached the body. "So this is the man you sent out to make sure the trail was safe," he sneered. "It would appear that it *is* safe. At least from space slugs."

"What happened to him?" Tash asked.

Jerec reached behind the miner's head and tugged at the hose connecting his air tank to his suit. It came away in two pieces.

"No air," the Imperial said.

Fandomar whispered, "What a terrible accident."

Jerec snorted. "This was no accident. Look at this air hose. It's been cut through by something sharp. A vibroblade or a laser torch." Jerec looked up. Even through his blindfold, he appeared to glare at them. "This man was murdered."

"But there's no one on the asteroid except us," Hoole said. "And we were all in the mining facility."

"Perhaps," Jerec said. "Perhaps not. I obviously should have brought more guards with me. All of you were out of my sight during at least part of our wait. So unless someone else has sneaked onto the asteroid, I'm sure one of you is a killer."

Tash shuddered as Jerec's skull-like face turned in her direction. She could feel his dark-side power sweep over her like a scanner. Then it passed on to Zak and Hoole.

Tash wondered who could have committed such a horrible act. If it wasn't Jerec himself (which was possible, she thought, since the Imperials had done worse things), then who? It obviously wasn't Zak or Uncle Hoole. Hodge and the other miner weren't likely suspects. Why would they kill their own friend, especially with so many witnesses around? That left only one person.

Fandomar.

Tash stole a glance at the Ithorian. She had certainly been acting strange since they'd discovered the warning and the tomb. Tash remembered how Fandomar had yelled, "No!" as Hodge tried to break through the sealed door. She'd seemed to know what would happen next. And once they were trapped, she had done nothing to help find a way out.

Then there was the connection between her husband and the Empire.

Whatever was happening, Tash thought, it was all connected to that strange room, or tomb, or whatever it was, at the bottom of the tunnel.

But Tash couldn't believe that Fandomar had killed the miner. Fandomar seemed so dedicated to the Ithorian Law of Life. Not only had she saved Zak from the vesuvague tree, but she had also defended the actions of the tree itself when Tash thought it should be destroyed.

Besides, Tash didn't get the same sort of dangerous feeling from Fandomar that she got from Jerec. She didn't know if it was her Force sensitivity or just plain common sense, but Tash could tell that Fandomar simply wasn't the kind of being who could kill.

These thoughts raced through her head as they traveled through the tunnel. Jerec did not wait for a glowrod—maybe he didn't need one. He walked ahead of the others, muttering, and soon was out of sight.

At the end of the tunnel, Tash could see indentations in the floor where the stone barrier had fallen. Beyond it stood the weird statue, and beyond that, the tomb. There was no sign of Jerec.

But the door stood open.

Cautiously, they approached the door. Hodge looked frustrated, like a man watching someone else steal his treasure. Fandomar didn't move at all. Hoole crept forward, with Zak and Tash right behind him.

In the silence of space, Tash thought she could hear her own heart pounding more loudly than a ship's engine. Hoole's words ran through her mind: *This tomb was not meant to be opened.*

But someone—Jerec?—had opened it.

Hoole reached the half-opened door. Carefully, he leaned inside to try to get a better look around. Suddenly, before Tash and Zak could even blink, something grabbed hold of Hoole and pulled him into the room!

Tash lunged forward without thinking, slipping through the doorway to help her uncle.

She didn't get a good look at the room beyond. She was too surprised at what she saw in front of her.

Jerec had grabbed the front of Hoole's tunic and lifted him off he ground with one hand. Tash realized that the Imperial must be immensely strong to overcome the force of the grav-boots with just one arm.

"Where is it?" Jerec demanded angrily.

Hoole's calm face stared directly into Jerec's. "I do not know what 'it' is. I told you, we are here by coincidence. I have no information."

Jerec looked as if he was trying to control his rage. Finally, he set Hoole down on the floor. Hoole's face remained calm, but Tash thought she detected an angry fire in her uncle's eyes.

"If I find out you were involved in this, I'll have you skinned alive," Jerec growled.

Hoole straightened the front of his spacesuit. "Perhaps if you tell me what has happened, I can be of service."

Jerec snarled and pointed to the center of the room. For the first time, Tash looked around. She was in a small circular chamber. The room was bare except for a pedestal in the very center.

"When I got here I found the door to the tomb open," Jerec snarled. "And it was completely empty!"

CHAPTER

8

As Jerec had stated, the tomb was bare. Tash could see that the pedestal had once held something, but the something had been removed.

Hoole considered. "Obviously, whoever murdered that miner came here and stole the contents of this room. Do you know what was here?"

Jerec sneered. "That is none of your concern."

By now the others had entered the room. Fandomar pushed her way past the others. Staring at the empty pedestal in wide-eyed horror, she let out a scream with her twin mouths that nearly shattered Tash's eardrums through the comlink. "Nnnnnnooooooooooo!"

Then Fandomar fainted.

It took a few minutes to revive her. When she came to her senses, Tash could see that her eyes were full of fear. They darted frantically from one person to the next. When Fandomar's eyes fell on her, Tash knew that Fandomar was *looking* for something. Not something on Tash's face, but something inside her. But she didn't know what.

"What is wrong with *you*?" Jerec demanded scornfully.

Fandomar studied Jerec carefully. Earlier, she had timidly avoided staring at him. Now she looked into his face. Again, Tash had the eerie feeling that Fandomar was trying to see something that was underneath Jerec's skin.

Finally, Fandomar answered in a whisper, "I'm sorry. I don't know what came over me. I apologize."

Jerec ignored Fandomar and turned to Hodge. He loomed threateningly over the chief miner as he growled, "And you. I delayed reaching this place on your advice. If I find out that you are involved with this, I'll have you vaporized."

Hodge only shrugged.

While Jerec raged and the others tried to console Fandomar, Hoole studied the pedestal. Like the statue, the pedestal was decorated with carved designs. These had been hastily scraped away, but again, just as at the statue, a few symbols remained.

"See anything, Uncle Hoole?" Tash asked.

Hoole studied the remaining symbols a moment longer. "I am not sure. Someone has gone to a great deal of trouble to remove any clues as to the nature of this tomb. But I suspect that there was never any treasure here. There are no indications that there were any containers or devices in here. If there was nothing valuable, why would anyone hide this room? Yet someone obviously thought it was important enough to kill for. For once," the Shi'ido admitted, "I seem to have more questions than answers."

"Speaking of questions," Zak added, "I have one. Has anyone else noticed the door?"

They all turned. Zak pointed at the heavy durasteel door that had sealed the tomb. Zak explained, "Look. The door opens outward, into the tunnel. But don't swinging doors usually open in, especially when they're locked?"

"Right!" Tash agreed. "Like in a house, the door opens in so that the people inside can lock it and keep strangers out."

Zak nodded furiously. "But this door opened into the tunnel. Which means that it wasn't designed to keep people out—"

"It was designed to keep something in," Tash said. Her face turned pale.

Hoole frowned. "And whatever it is, it is now free."

Tash felt a cold shadow pass over her and realized

that Jerec was standing behind her. She shuddered, wondering if he could sense her tiny Force power the way she could feel his dark side.

"Your detective work bores me," the Imperial sneered. "And it is not needed here. I suggest you end it. Or I shall end it for you."

The stormtrooper fingered his blaster, leaving no doubt in Tash's mind just how Jerec would end things.

Jerec led them back to the mining facility at a rapid pace. Again, the stormtrooper brought up the rear . . . but this time Tash felt sure he was waiting eagerly for Jerec's order to shoot them all in the back.

They passed the body of the miner, still held in place by his grav-boots. Hodge and the other miner wanted to take the body with them, but Jerec refused to let them stop.

Tash stared straight ahead, fixing her eyes on the mining colony in the distance. It was the only safe place to look. She dared not glance up, where the storm of asteroids continued to spin crazily in the darkness of space. Looking to either side, all she could see was the lifeless rock of the asteroid. And behind her marched Jerec's stormtrooper.

She found herself wishing she were back on Ithor. The forest had been so beautiful, so full of life. Remembering her brief experience with the Bafforr trees, she felt a warm glow spread through her, right down to her fingertips. She suddenly felt stifled inside the bulky spacesuit. She felt trapped. She wanted to get out of this place. Everything would be all right if she could just get off the asteroid.

But until then, the closest thing to safety was the mining colony. Then they could take the cargo ship back to Ithor. If Jerec didn't kill them outright, or discover who they were first.

Finally they reached the airlock that led into the miners' outpost. Jerec's other stormtrooper was waiting there. By the time Tash stepped through the airlock, Jerec, Hoole, and Zak were already inside the docking bay. Although they all still had their space helmets on, Zak had removed his grav-boots.

"I always wondered what it was like to fly!" he joked. He kicked his feet off the ground and floated toward the ceiling. "This is prime!"

"I'm repressurizing the airlock," Hodge said, once everyone was inside. He pulled a large handle. There was soft click, a rush of air . . .

. . . and an enormous explosion.

CHAPTER

Tash and the others were thrown to the floor as a loud *BOOM!* echoed inside their space helmets. The deafening sound seemed to go on forever.

Then Tash realized that the sound she heard wasn't a continuing explosion—it was the howling of air rushing out of the airlock. The explosion had blown a hole through the airlock door, and the sealed atmosphere of the mining facility was now being sucked into space.

"Helmets on!" Hoole commanded. Tash had just started to remove hers, and had barely snapped it back into place before the wind tried to tear it right off her head.

The howling wind tugged at her, but she quickly grabbed hold of a metal rail along the wall. The combination of her tight grip and the grav-boots held her in place. The others, too, grabbed hold of the closest thing they could find to keep from being sucked out of the airlock.

Zak was not so lucky.

He had still been floating in the zero-gravity room without his boots when the explosion happened. He hovered in the air long enough to make eye contact with his sister before the wind grabbed him with great force and sent him tumbling through the hole in the wall.

"Zak!" Tash screamed. Releasing her grip on the railing, she let the powerful wind push her toward the hole, the grav-boots slowing her movements. When she reached the hole, she braced herself on the wall and looked out into space. By the time she spotted him, Zak was a small white dot tumbling head over heels into the asteroid field.

"Tash, help!" she heard Zak's voice inside her helmet's comlink.

Then he vanished from sight.

Tash turned to the nearest person, Jerec, and pleaded, "We've got to help him!"

Jerec ignored her. He had hardly noticed Zak's disappearance. The Imperial was scanning the room. "The Ithorian," he muttered. "That Ithorian is missing." He turned to his stormtroopers. "This must be her doing. Find her! I want that Hammerhead!"

Most of the mining station's air had escaped by now. With less oxygen sealed inside the walls, there was less pressure, and the wind died down. By the time the two stormtroopers churned into motion, there was hardly a breeze left, and then nothing at all.

The stormtroopers opened the inner door of the airlock and hurried into the facility with Jerec close behind them.

That left Hoole, Tash, and the two miners. But Hodge and his partner were unwilling to help. "We've got to try to contain this explosion. We've got a fortune in minerals in this place!" the chief miner apologized as they hurried out of the room.

"Uncle Hoole, what do we do?" Tash started to ask. She stopped. Hoole was already halfway to the row of yellow Starflies parked along one wall.

"I've never flown one of these before!" she said as her uncle climbed into the nearest craft.

"Neither have I," Hoole replied grimly. "I suspect Zak would tell us we were going to take a crash course. Get in."

Tash jumped into another of the tiny ships. She was surprised to find the cockpit was quite large—until she remembered that the Starfly didn't carry its own oxygen. The pilot had to wear space gear, so the designers had added extra room to fit the bulky suits.

The controls were basic, and Tash had the engines fired up in seconds. "Tash, do you copy?" Hoole's calm voice came over the comlink. It steadied her trembling hands.

"Yes," she said into the microphone. "What are we going to do?"

"We must fly into the asteroids and grab him with the ship's tractor beams, just as the miners rescued us," her uncle explained.

We must fly into the asteroids.

Tash shuddered. It was bad enough to have the asteroids rocketing through the sky over her head. Flying through them—that was like daring the space rocks to smash them.

Hoole seemed to read her thoughts. "Don't worry, Tash. Starflies were made for this type of work. Keep your eyes open and trust your skills. Let's go."

Hoole's Starfly lifted off the deck and accelerated toward the hole in the wall.

For an instant, Tash was frozen. She tried to force her hands to work the controls, but they wouldn't move.

Think of Zak, she told herself. She took a deep breath, the kind that had always made her feel calm. Relaxed. Closer to the Force.

Her hands moved.

Before she knew it, her Starfly had slipped out of the docking bay and was rising from the asteroid's surface. She could see Hoole's ship like a bright yellow dot against the black field of space. She hit her thrusters and sped to catch up.

Suddenly, an asteroid the size of a bantha dropped into view, tumbling toward her viewscreen. The Starfly seemed to leap out of the asteroid's path with a mind of its own.

Tash looked down at her controls. She had moved the ship without thinking! Her arms tingled. Wasn't this how she'd felt in the past when she'd used the Force? And wasn't it just how she'd felt when she tried to talk to the Bafforr trees?

Tash moved the controls again, and her Starfly looped easily around the next space rock.

She almost laughed out loud. She felt as if she were playing speed globe again. Only now she was the globe, and all the asteroids were trying to catch her!

It's like I can predict where they're coming from and where they're going, she thought. *Almost like . . . I'm connected to them.*

Tash knew that the Force was an energy field that connected all living things. Did it apply to space rocks, too?

More than ever, she wished that someone could answer her questions. She wished . . .

Whatever she wished, she forgot it the next instant, as her eyes fell on a small white object turning slow circles toward a giant asteroid—an asteroid even larger than the one the miners lived on. The surface of the asteroid was covered in holes and caverns. In one of those caverns, Tash could see a space slug huddling, its mouth slowly opening and closing like that of a fish in water.

The small white object was Zak.

He was heading right into the space slug's mouth.

CHAPTER

10

Zak was about to be swallowed by the space slug.

Tash felt the tingling sensation leave her body. The asteroids that had seemed easy to dodge a moment ago swirled around her again. She jerked the controls hard to avoid one rock and nearly smashed into another.

"Uncle Hoole, help!" she called out.

"Stay calm, Tash," the Shi'ido's steady voice replied. "I'll distract the space slug while you try to grab hold of Zak."

"I—I can't!"

There was a pause. Then Hoole said, "Yes, you can. A moment ago you were flying this asteroid field like it was an obstacle course back on the playground on Alderaan. You can do it."

Tash felt her palms start to sweat, but since they were

trapped inside her gloves, she had no way to wipe them dry. Hoole was right. She could do it. She *had* to do it.

There was no time left to be afraid. The space slug lunged out of its hole toward Zak.

Hoole's Starfly tilted its nose toward the space slug and fired its thrusters, diving toward the creature. Its lasers fired, sending two beams of white-hot energy into the giant worm's hide. It was like pricking a bantha with a needle, but the shots distracted the worm enough to make it swerve aside, looking for whatever had attacked it. Jaws that could crush an Imperial walker chomped down just as Hoole slipped out of its way.

Sprranng!

Tash felt something bounce off the side of her Starfly and thanked the Force that it had only been a mini-asteroid. Anything larger would have crushed her. Taking a deep breath, she punched her thrusters to full power and shot toward her brother.

An asteroid seemed to appear out of nowhere. She turned her ship in a tight spin and slipped around it.

Two asteroids headed right for one another. Tash eased off her thrusters as the rocks collided in front of her.

But the two smashed asteroids had turned into a hundred smaller rocks. There was no way to avoid them. Tash closed her eyes tight and moved her control stick, flying totally by feel.

When she opened her eyes, she'd passed through the debris untouched.

Zak was right in front of her now. She was close enough to see his arms waving helplessly in the void. She could see his frightened eyes. They were as wide as a Rodian's. But they weren't staring at Tash. They were staring into the mouth of the space slug. As wide and bottomless as a black hole, it reached out as Zak hurtled forward.

"Activating tractor beam," Tash said, reaching for the right button without even knowing it.

A beam of pale white light reached out from her Starfly and touched Zak. Instantly, her brother stopped his tumble through space.

The space slug's jaws slammed down less than a dozen meters from Zak. If the tractor beam hadn't caught him, Zak would have been on the inside of its mouth rather than the outside.

Hoole's Starfly flashed into view, blasters blazing. Energy bolts pounded the space slug's head. It thrashed about angrily for a moment, then retreated into its cave.

Tash found the control knob that pulled the tractor beam in, drawing Zak toward her ship. "Zak, do you copy?" she asked into her comlink.

"Y-Yeah," came a weak, trembling voice. "But I think I've had enough spacewalking for one day."

Using the tractor beam, Tash drew her brother toward her ship until he could reach out and touch the hull.

Quickly, she popped open the top of her Starfly and pulled him inside. "Is there room?" he asked.

"I think so," she replied. "There's some space behind the seat. Curl up back there. And hurry. I want to get out of here before another asteroid comes our way."

They reached the mining facility in minutes, with Hoole flying just behind them. When they landed, they were surprised to find that the Starflies Jerec and his men had used to reach the asteroid were gone. The Imperials had left the asteroid and returned to their Star Destroyer.

A low rumble in the rock beneath their feet told them why. "The asteroid's unstable after that explosion," said Hodge as they walked into the main room. He and his partner, still wearing their spacesuits, were stuffing a few personal items into travel packs. Fandomar sat in a corner, nervously adjusting her space helmet.

Hodge went on: "We're safe for a few minutes, but we've got to evacuate immediately."

"Can we take off our spacesuits now?" Zak asked.

"No!" Fandomar almost shouted.

Hodge explained, "The explosion knocked out the environmental controls. There's no air."

"What caused the explosion?" Hoole asked. He glanced at Fandomar. "Jerec seemed to think it was sabotage."

Hodge shrugged. "Hard to tell. Could have been a malfunction or sabotage."

Tash couldn't help asking, "Fandomar . . . where were you during the explosion?"

"I—I was—" the Ithorian stammered, "I was . . . a-alone."

Tash swallowed. That wasn't much of an alibi.

Hodge, however, didn't seem concerned about who might have set off the explosion. "All I care about now is getting off this rock and down to Ithor. Fandomar's going to take us."

The six survivors hurried aboard Fandomar's cargo ship as the Ithorian sealed the hatch. "Don't remove your spacesuits," she warned. "I managed to repair the damage done by the space slug, but this explosion has caused a loss of environmental controls. No air. Your suits must stay on until we reach Ithor."

"Great," Zak groaned, dropping down into a flight chair. "I'll never get out of this suit."

"Tash, Zak, would you come with me, please?" Hoole asked.

The two Arrandas followed their uncle out of the cockpit. Behind the pilot's room lay one small cargo hold, then another larger one beyond that. Hoole passed through each cargo hold, shutting the doors tightly behind him. When they reached the back of the ship, Hoole spoke into his comlink. "Fandomar? Fandomar, do you copy?"

When there was no answer, he nodded. "Good. The cargo doors are blocking the signal, so she can't hear us.'' He looked at his niece and nephew. ''Tash, Zak, I am afraid we must consider an unpleasant possibility.'' He paused. ''Fandomar may be a murderer.''

''No!'' Tash replied. ''She couldn't be. She's too gentle.''

Hoole nodded. ''I know how she seems. But she is the only being without an alibi for the time the miner was murdered.''

Tash shook her head. ''Hodge and the other miner were out of sight, too.''

Zak shrugged. ''Yeah, but why would they kill their own partner? Especially with Imperials in the neighborhood?''

Hoole agreed with Zak. ''And Fandomar was the only person not present when the explosion occurred. She must have slipped away as soon as we returned to the mining facility.''

''But why would she kill someone? And blow up the miners' station?'' Tash asked.

Her uncle replied, ''I do not know. All of this is somehow connected to the tomb on the asteroid. Something was kept at the bottom of that tunnel. I am not sure what it was, but I have at least a few clues.''

Tash and Zak listened closely as their uncle lowered his voice even more. ''The writing on the inner chamber was somewhat clearer than on the sign at the base of the statue. I read the word *Spore*.''

''Spore?'' Zak asked. ''What's that? A person?''

"I'm not sure," the Shi'ido admitted. "But there were dates written on the inner room as well. They were nearly destroyed, but I believe they match the dates Tash mentioned. The dates when all Ithorian records were missing."

Zak wrinkled his brow. "I'm getting a headache. So we've got a mysterious time in history the Ithorians didn't want to record, and something called Spore buried on an asteroid. Then we have an Imperial who wants this Spore, a miner who gets murdered for it, and an explosion that drives everyone off the asteroid."

"Do not forget," Hoole added, "that Fandomar volunteered to fly the shuttle from the planet to the asteroid. That meant that she could keep her eye on the miners . . ."

"To see if they discovered the tomb!" Zak finished. "Of course! She knows what this Spore is and wants it for herself."

Tash clicked her tongue in frustration. "She's an Ithorian. What about the Law of Life?"

"We must remember that Fandomar's husband has already disobeyed Ithorian law," Hoole replied. "He gave secrets to the Empire. Fandomar may be equally unpredictable."

Tash didn't agree.

"I just don't believe it," she said stubbornly.

"Help!" a voice suddenly shouted loudly enough to be picked up by their comlinks.

Tash, Zak, and Hoole rushed toward the front of the ship in time to see that one of the ship's hatches had been opened. Stars twinkled in the darkness beyond.

Fandomar stood in the doorway, shoving one of the miners out into the void.

CHAPTER

The miner's fingers clung desperately to the edges of the hatch. He tried to pull himself back into the ship, but Fandomar grabbed hold of his hands and pried them loose. Not until that moment did Tash realize that the long, delicate Ithorian fingers were also incredibly strong.

"Help! Help!" the miner cried, but it was too late. He was kicked free of the ship's hull. Even on sublight drive, the cargo ship was traveling incredibly fast. He was floating through space ten kilometers behind the ship before anyone could move.

Hoole drew a blaster from the pouch in his spacesuit. Briefly, Tash wondered where he'd gotten it. Her uncle almost never used weapons. He usually relied on his incredible shape-shifting ability in time of need. But she guessed that his power was as limited here as it had been near the asteroid tomb.

"Do not move," the Shi'ido said, his voice like hard stone.

Fandomar hardly looked at the blaster. "He'll be fine, he'll be fine!" she said, almost to herself. "He's got enough oxygen in his tank to last almost twenty-four hours. We can send a rescue ship out to get him as soon as we reach the planet."

This took Tash totally by surprise. She could see that it had shocked her uncle, too. "If you want to rescue him, why throw him off the ship in the first place?" Hoole asked.

"Oooohhhhh."

A low moan came from the floor near their feet. Tash saw that Hodge lay in the corner. Moving awkwardly in his bulky spacesuit, the chief miner staggered to his feet. He shook his head and muttered, "S-Somebody dropped sleeping gas into my air tank."

Tash felt her face turn red, and a hot tear welled up in her eye. She didn't know whether to be embarrassed or horrified or angry or all three at once. "You were going to kill Hodge, too," she whispered. "Were we next?"

Fandomar shook her head. She was crying. The sobbing from her twin throats was pitifully sad. "I—I haven't killed anyone. And I wouldn't have touched you, Tash. I knew it couldn't be any of you. You were in the mining facility the whole time."

"What whole time?" Zak asked.

Hoole kept his blaster steady on the Ithorian. "Fandomar, I think it is time you told us what is happening here."

Fandomar's two mouths trembled. "It's Spore," she whispered.

A soft alarm sounded. "It is nothing," Hoole said, sparing a quick glance at the instrument panel. "We are entering the Ithorian atmosphere."

The instant he looked away, Fandomar bolted for the cockpit.

"Uncle Hoole!" Tash warned.

Hoole pointed his blaster at Fandomar's back. But he didn't fire. Tash knew her uncle couldn't shoot anyone in the back.

They were only a few steps behind her, but in those few seconds Fandomar slammed into the controls, tearing at the control stick and smashing the scanner screens with her gloved hands. The ship's nose tilted up and everyone tumbled forward against the console as the cargo carrier went into a steep dive.

Tash and Zak grabbed Fandomar's arms, trying to drag her back from the controls. Hodge staggered up behind them and grabbed the back of Fandomar's spacesuit. Much stronger than the two Arrandas, he was able to haul Fandomar away from the pilot's seat.

Instantly, Hoole took her place. He pulled back on

the control stick, but the ship responded sluggishly. Fandomar had damaged the flight-control system.

On the viewscreen, they could see the nose of the ship plunge out of dark space into the blue sky of Ithor. The green planet rushed up to meet them.

Hoole worked like a machine, running through every option. He tried the thrusters. He worked the repulsor engines. He diverted power from the ship's deflector shields. Nothing worked. The ship barely responded to his commands.

The front of the falling cargo ship turned white-hot. They were falling so fast, they had caught fire.

Tash couldn't even scream—her heart was pounding in her throat. "Seats!" she heard her uncle rasp. For a second she didn't know what he meant. Then she realized she wasn't buckled in to anything. Frantically, she let go of Fandomar, dropped into the nearest chair, and strapped herself into the crashwebbing. Beside her, Zak had done the same thing.

Something bumped against Tash's leg. The speed globe. She picked it up and nervously held the soft globe tight as the ship continued to fall.

Tash told herself they would be all right. Hoole would never give up. He was too calm, too capable to give up. The Shi'ido always found a way out of the most desperate situation.

She watched Hoole work until the last second, hoping he would find some trick that would bring the ship out of its dive. Then her heart sank. Hoole removed his hands from the controls and covered his head. "Brace yourselves," he said. "We're going to crash!"

The cargo ship slammed into the dense forest of Ithor.

CHAPTER 12

Tash felt something soft and warm beneath her. It felt like a mattress.

I'm lying on a bed, she thought. *I must be in my cabin. This has all been a dream.*

She rolled over onto her other side and felt her face bump against a piece of sharp metal. "Ow!" she muttered drowsily. She opened her eyes.

The sharp metal object was the comlink microphone in her space helmet. A long, jagged crack ran from the top of the helmet's faceplate to the bottom.

Tash sat up with a start, then lay back down with a moan. Her head was ringing. She'd gotten up too fast and made herself dizzy. She waited for the forest around her to stop spinning, then sat up slowly.

The mattress she'd been lying on was a thick bed of

moss at the foot of an enormous Bafforr tree. As she rose to her knees, Tash felt bruises forming all over her body. The dizziness had stopped, but her head still ached. She must have taken a blow to the head during the crash. Where her visor was not cracked, it was covered in smears of mossy slime. Unclipping the helmet's seals, she popped it off and tossed the headgear into the brush.

The ship was nowhere in sight, but Tash sniffed the scent of burning ozone and engine exhaust, so she knew it was close by. The speed globe she'd been holding lay a couple of meters away.

"I must have been thrown clear when we hit," she said, mostly to make sure her sore jaw still worked. "If I hadn't landed on this moss, I would have broken my neck."

Sitting back down, Tash kicked off her grav-boots, then unsealed her spacesuit and shook it off. In zero gravity, the suit was weightless, but planetside it was almost too heavy to lift.

Tash tried to stand up, using the Bafforr tree for support.

The minute her hand touched the dark, smooth bark of the tree, an electric tingle shot up her arm and into her brain. A single word echoed loudly in her mind.

Danger!

Instinctively, Tash ducked back down.

At the same moment, she heard a loud rustling in the

bushes nearby. Crouched down in the underbrush, she couldn't see a thing, but she heard heavy footsteps clomp past only a few meters from her hiding spot. The warning message had been so clear that she didn't dare look up until the sound of movement faded among the trees.

When the forest had been silent a long time, Tash stood up again. Cautiously, she touched the tree.

Nothing happened.

Had the warning been a message from the Bafforr tree? Or the Force? Or both?

Another possibility occurred to Tash. She could still hear a soft ringing in her ears, and she had to admit that the danger signal might have been a trick of her rattled brain. She might have just hidden from a chance at being rescued.

Tash thought about shouting for help. She opened her mouth and filled her lungs with air, but something held her back. Instead she let out a long sigh.

Her sigh was answered by a pain-filled moan from beneath the vines of a nearby blue-flowered shrub.

Tash approached the shrub cautiously. The last thing she needed was to be snared by another of Ithor's hungry plants. But this one seemed harmless enough. She could see a figure lying motionless at its roots. Drawing nearer, Tash saw that it was Fandomar.

Tash staggered to the Ithorian's side and carefully turned her over. Fandomar's spacesuit was torn, probably by a tree branch as she was thrown clear of the wreck. A nasty cut ran the length of her leg. Her helmet had been cracked in two and nearly torn from her neck. Tash popped it off and threw it aside.

"Fandomar?" she whispered gently. "Fandomar, can you hear me?"

The Ithorian's eyes fluttered open, then closed again. "T-Tash. Is that you? I can't seem to focus my eyes." She tried to move. "I can't feel my legs, either."

"It's me," Tash replied. "Lie still. We were both thrown clear of the wreckage. You're probably pretty banged up."

A look of panic suddenly crossed Fandomar's face, and her hands clutched blindly at Tash. "Tash, your voice. It doesn't sound like it's coming through the comlink. You're not wearing your helmet?"

"No. Neither are you. We're on Ithor."

"Oh, no, no, no, no," Fandomar moaned. "This is terrible."

Tash blinked. Her head hurt too much to deal with this confusion. "What are you talking about?"

"Spore," Fandomar hissed. She said the word as if it were the most terrible thing in the galaxy. "Spore! Spore is free!"

"What do you mean?" Tash asked.

Fandomar started to cry. "It means," she wept, "we're all doomed!"

CHAPTER 13

"Doomed!" Fandomar whispered again. Her voice was fading.

"What is this Spore?" Tash asked. "Fandomar, you have to tell me!"

But the Ithorian had fainted.

Tash wanted to shake her awake, but she dared not. Fandomar had said she couldn't feel her legs. Her spine might be broken. If Tash moved her, she could make the damage worse.

I'll have to leave her here, Tash decided. *Maybe I can get help.*

Tash used a jagged piece of metal from Fandomar's helmet to tear strips of cloth from the Ithorian's spacesuit. She used these to bandage Fandomar's leg wound. Then she used the rest of the suit as a blanket to cover the Hammerhead's body. That was the best she could do.

She needed to find Hoole and Zak and make sure they were all right. Then maybe they could find a way to contact the *Tafanda Bay*.

Tash staggered through the forest of Bafforr trees. She had to stop every ten meters or so to catch her breath and let the ringing in her ears quiet down. Every time she rested against a Bafforr's trunk, she waited for that same tingle of energy. But it never came, even when Tash heard loud rustling in the bushes nearby.

Tash braced herself and waited. Something big and heavy-footed pushed its way through the bushes before her.

A tall gray figure stepped into view.

"Uncle Hoole!" Tash shouted in pure joy. She threw herself at the Shi'ido, who almost lost his footing. Tash saw a deep cut on his forehead.

"Are you injured?" he asked.

She wasn't sure. "I'm one big bruise and my ears are ringing, but I'm okay. Is your cut bad?"

Hoole touched the gash delicately. "I will live." The stern Shi'ido tried to look as light hearted as his stony face could manage. "It was not my best landing, but all things considered, I would say it wasn't my worst."

Tash grimaced. Hoole never joked. The fact that he was trying to probably meant he felt worse than he looked. "Fandomar is back there in the forest. She's hurt. Do you think the Ithorians saw the crash on their scanners? Will they send a rescue party?''

''I think the answer is yes,'' said Zak as he slipped between the branches of a sapling tree. Tash couldn't see any cuts or bruises, but her brother's knees were wobbly. He hugged Tash and Hoole as he said, ''I saw a ship fly overhead. The crash site's just on the other side of these trees. They'll probably land there.''

Zak was right. The three survivors helped each other through the trees and into a clearing. The twisted wreckage of the cargo ship lay piled at the end of a long gouged-out trail it had dug into the ground.

Tash looked back, trying to guess how far she'd walked, and silently thanked the Force. She'd been thrown an incredible distance from the ship. How had she survived? That moss had been soft, but not soft enough to save her from cracking her skull after being launched a hundred meters.

A look of wonder and suspicion crossed her face. She'd been thrown through a grove of Bafforr trees. Had the trees somehow—?

Tash shook her head. Force or no Force, she couldn't believe that the trees had saved her.

Thoughts of a miraculous rescue were driven out as real rescuers appeared. A small medical shuttle dropped down almost at their feet, and four Ithorians carrying medi-pacs jumped out of the hatch. In seconds they were examining all three survivors, treating Hoole's head wound, and testing Tash to make sure she didn't have a concussion from her fall.

"You've got to help Fandomar," Tash insisted. "She's back there, through the trees."

One of the medics nodded. "Let us make sure you are well first, then you can lead us to her."

"I'm fine!" Tash insisted. But she didn't feel fine. Her ears had stopped ringing, but that sensation had been replaced by another. It was as if a long-range sensor had triggered a warning inside her head.

Something was *wrong*.

"Hey, I could use some help, too!" said a gruff voice.

Hodge stepped out of the shade of a Bafforr tree. He had shed his spacesuit and helmet and walked forward wearing only a miner's jumpsuit and a wide grin. There wasn't a scratch on him.

"Fandomar needs help badly," Tash said. "I left her back there. Her back may be injured, and I think she's delirious. She kept saying something about everyone being doomed. And she mentioned Spore."

All four Ithorians froze. In a frightened whisper, one of them said, "What?"

The fear in their eyes made Tash shiver. "I said she talked about Spore. What does that mean?"

None of the Ithorians answered. Hodge laughed coldly. "I'm afraid that what she means," he said, "is me!"

In the next instant, Hodge turned on the closest person—an Ithorian doctor who had started to examine him. What happened then was beyond Tash's imagination.

Hodge's eyes seemed to explode with thin, dark, vinelike tentacles. More dark vines burst from his open mouth. They lashed out violently, wrapping themselves around the doctor and sinking right into the Ithorian's skin!

CHAPTER 14

The dark tentacles sank into the Ithorian's skin, burying themselves inside the victim's body. Tash blinked. The tentacles vanished from sight except for a dark tracing of lines, like veins, that showed beneath the skin.

But the Ithorian himself had changed. His body stiffened and he seemed to be waiting for something.

"What was that?" Zak asked.

"Spore!" one of the Ithorians gasped in a voice filled with terror.

"I am Spore," said Hodge and the Hammerhead together. Hodge grinned, and he and the Ithorian spoke again. "For years, for centuries, I have been trapped on that lifeless rock. In that airless tomb! At last I have lives to feed on again!"

As one being, Hodge and the Ithorian turned on the other three Hammerheads and opened their mouths. More black tendrils erupted from their mouths and eyes, snaring the three Ithorian doctors. In the midst of her horror, Tash thought the black strings looked like the roots of a fast-growing weed.

Spore had now captured all the Ithorians.

Spore and his victims turned on Hoole. "You are next to join me," Spore said.

A whole forest of tentacles leaped out to capture Hoole. But Hoole had vanished. In the Shi'ido's place appeared a crystal snake. The slithering creature twisted and squirmed, slipping out of the tangle of black tentacles. Quick as a light beam, the crystal snake dodged to one side. Its skin crawled quickly across its body, and Hoole appeared again.

His dodge had carried him to the other side of the clearing. Spore stood between the Arrandas and the Shi'ido.

"Run!" Hoole ordered; then he plunged into the forest.

With no other choice, Zak and Tash fled in the opposite direction.

They ran blindly, jumping over tree roots, ducking under branches, scrambling up small hillocks. The horrible vision of those black vines bursting out of Hodge's mouth made their feet move long after they were exhausted.

Finally, Tash's tired feet tripped her up and she top-pled down a gentle, grass-covered slope. Zak fell right behind her, and they came to a stop at the feet of an-other grove of trees. They rested against the dark trunk of a Bafforr tree.

"Wh-Wh-What . . . ?" Zak panted. He didn't need to finish his sentence.

"Spore," Tash answered. "That's what was trapped on the asteroid."

"And Fandomar let it loose?" her brother guessed.

Tash shook her head, almost too tired to speak. "I don't think it was her. I think it was Hodge. It infected him somehow, took him over. Now he's infecting ev-eryone else."

"Every time those vine-things touch someone, it's like they become part of Spore," Zak said. "It's like they're suddenly all connected."

Tash shuddered. "What do we do?"

"Find Uncle Hoole," her brother suggested.

"Right," she agreed. "Then find a way to warn the *Tafanda Bay*. Whatever this thing is, the Ithorians seem to know about it."

"That's what scares me," Zak said with a shake of his head. "Did you see how scared *they* were?"

"But they trapped it once before," his sister replied. "Maybe they can do it again."

Suddenly, Tash stiffened.

"Tash, what's wrong?"

She didn't answer at first. Sitting with her back to a Bafforr tree, she had felt the warning signal even more powerfully than before.

DANGER!

"They're near," she whispered. "Come on."

Getting to their feet, Zak and Tash slipped behind the tree as quietly as possible, then backed deeper into the grove of Bafforrs. Zak didn't know how Tash knew Spore was close, but he had trusted her feelings in the past. This didn't seem like a good time to start doubting her.

Tash felt her mouth go dry. The feeling of dread continued to pulse through her brain. Danger was in the air around her.

Hoole appeared at the top of the hill down which they'd fallen. He hurried down the slope toward them, his eyes scanning the trees and underbrush.

"Uncle Hoole!" Tash whispered when he had gotten within earshot. "Over here!"

The Shi'ido's head whipped around the minute he heard her voice. A few quick strides carried him right up to the tree that hid them.

"Zak, Tash, I am glad I found you," Hoole said.

Tash beckoned him into the shadow of the tree. "Uncle Hoole, you've got to hide. Spore is very near. Come on!"

Hoole shook his head. He smiled and held out his hand. "No, no, Tash. Everything is fine. Join me."

Zak stepped out from behind the tree and toward his uncle's waiting hand. Tash started to follow, then froze.

Join me.

The way he'd said those words reminded her of something.

As Zak approached his uncle, the Shi'ido opened his mouth in a wide grin.

The black vines snared Zak before he could even scream.

Tash stumbled backward. The tendrils melted into Zak's body, leaving only black lines visible beneath the skin around his neck. She thought she might be sick.

Hoole and Zak didn't follow as she took a few steps back. Instead, they held up their hands innocently and said at the same time, "Tash, please don't run."

Danger!

The warning pulsed all around her. Tash could feel her heart slam against her ribs, and hear the blood pound in her ears. She knew she should run. But this was Hoole. That was Zak. How could she run?

She tried to keep her voice from shaking as she asked, "Who are you?"

"I am Spore," said Zak and Hoole together. The sound of their voices had the same stereo effect as an

Ithorian voice. "I mean you no harm. I simply need . . . I mean, I *want* to know you better. To be a part of you. For you to be a part of me."

The phrase chilled Tash's heart. Spore's words reminded her of the feeling she'd gotten before the Bafforr trees, only turned inside out. Instead of feeling the soothing presence of the wise trees trying to connect with her, she felt a dark, evil presence that wanted to control her.

She stared closely at the spiderweb of dark lines hiding beneath Zak's skin and choked back a sob.

"First," she managed to say, "let go of my brother. Let go of Uncle Hoole."

"I will, I promise," Spore replied through Hoole and Zak. "But I need them at the moment. They're going to help me. I promise you, none of you will come to any harm."

"You're already harming them," she said.

"Only because I was desperate," Spore said. "I was trapped for four hundred years. I needed to be free. Once I'm sure I'll be free, then I'll release anyone who doesn't want to be a part of me."

Hoole and Zak took a few steps closer. When they spoke, their voices seemed to change, relaxing into their natural speech. But they still spoke together. "Tash, it's not bad. Won't you join us?"

Tash took another uncertain step back and her foot

slipped on the root of the Bafforr tree. Instinctively, she grabbed the tree trunk for balance.

Run!

The message thundered through her mind, too powerful to ignore. Her feet were moving before her brain could form the thought.

She barely saw the black strings slap harmlessly against the tree behind her.

Tash ran for her life. Branches slapped at her face, scratching tears from her eyes. But she wasn't crying from the pain. She was crying out of fear.

How could Zak and Uncle Hoole have been caught? How could she escape Spore all alone?

Alone. She was tired of being alone. Even when she was with her uncle and her brother, she felt different from them. She thought the Force was supposed to make her feel *connected* to everything, but at the moment she felt like the loneliest, most frightened being in the galaxy. She kept moving, but her legs began to feel heavy. Her lungs started to ache.

Why bother running? she told herself. *What good will it do you? You're running from the only friends you have.*

Tash stopped to catch her breath in a clearing. After a moment, she saw that the bushes all around her were alive with movement. Pulling aside the branches, she saw an Ithorian, one of the medical staff, scanning the forest. It took a few steps forward, looked around, then advanced again. She could hear Spore's other victims all around her, doing the same.

She was caught in the middle of a circle. There was nowhere to run. Soon they'd find her. She looked up. There were Bafforr trees all around her, but the lowest branches were far too high for her to reach. And the bark of the trunk was far too slick for her to try to shimmy up the side.

She glanced down—and saw something familiar.

Her spacesuit.

She was back where she started. Not that it would do her any good. There were no weapons in her spacesuit. Just the air tank, the helmet, and . . .

. . . and grav-boots.

Tash looked back at the nearest Bafforr tree. There was no way to climb it. But what if she could *walk* up the side of the tree instead?

The rustling in the bushes was very close.

It might work, but she needed time to get the grav-boots on her feet.

Tash looked around desperately, until her eyes were caught by a flash of red.

The speed globe.

She had been holding it when the ship crashed. Scooping it up now, she flipped the activation switch and thanked the Force as the speed globe hummed to life.

She could hear someone approaching from her left. It was the Ithorian medic she'd seen earlier.

Tash flicked another switch and the speed globe jumped out of her hands, bouncing onto the forest floor. "Get going!" she rasped, stomping her foot in the globe's direction. The computerized ball bounced away into the underbrush.

Whoever had been approaching from Tash's left suddenly stopped, listening as the speed globe bounced through the bushes before it, too, stopped.

The Ithorian started forward, but as it approached the speed globe's location, the ball shot away, making more noise in the brush.

The Ithorian followed.

While this had been happening, Tash hadn't wasted a moment. As fast as she could, she slipped on her grav-boots. As soon as the buckles were snapped, she hurried toward the nearest tree—and nearly fell on her face.

She'd forgotten how heavy the boots were.

Picking herself up, she dragged her feet to the trunk. She lifted one foot and planted it against the smooth black bark. Then, with a silent hope that the Force was with her, she activated the grav-boot.

The mini–tractor beam powered up, and she felt her foot clamp down. It worked! Quickly, she hopped up and stuck her other foot onto the trunk.

Then, step by step, Tash walked up the side of the Bafforr tree.

It wasn't easy. Even though her feet stuck to the trunk, gravity still pulled her body toward the ground. She had to use all the muscles in her legs to keep herself from bending backward like a branch too heavy with blumfruit.

Tash had just reached the lowest level of branches when she heard several sets of footsteps burst out of the brush beneath her, converging on the spot where she'd been standing. She froze, trying not to make a sound.

Below her, Zak, Hoole, and the Ithorians had gathered around Hodge. One of the Ithorians held up the speed globe. Hodge took it, then dropped it on the ground in disgust. None of them spoke. Tash suspected that they didn't need to. They were all thinking with one mind—Spore's.

Tash hoped that the branches around her would hide her from sight, but the Spore-victims didn't even look up. The Bafforr tree would have been impossible to climb.

Tash's legs started to tremble. Inside the grav-boots, her ankles ached.

A moment later, the victims of Spore dispersed, hunting the ground for any sign of their next prey.

Tash forced herself to walk a few feet to the nearest thick branch and crawled onto it. As soon as she had caught her breath, she looked around, trying to figure out her next move. She had to warn the *Tafanda Bay,* or any other herd ship she could find.

First things first, though. She had to get safely away from Spore. But how?

The answer came to Tash so quickly and easily that she almost laughed. She didn't know if she'd figured it out for herself, or if it was the Force, or if it was yet another message from the Bafforr trees. All three seemed to be getting mixed together. Whichever it was, the solution popped into her mind as a single word.

Connections.

Just as the Bafforrs seemed to be connected as one mind, their branches had grown close together, sometimes touching, sometimes intertwining so that at the tops, one tree could hardly be distinguished from the next.

Tash crawled along the branch she was sitting on until she reached the branch of the nearest tree. Carefully, she switched trees, and continued on her way. Sometimes she had to climb down to reach a good branch; sometimes she climbed up. It wasn't easy. Within minutes her hands, arms, and legs were scratched, but slowly, she covered distance.

Wherever Spore thought she was, that wasn't where she was going to be soon. Tash allowed herself a momentary smile.

Then the smile vanished. The branch she had just climbed onto suddenly wrapped itself around her body and pulled her down toward the ground. More branches snared her arms and legs.

She had crawled into the vines of a vesuvague tree.

CHAPTER

16

Tash struggled, but she knew it was no use. The tree was too strong. It had pulled her down from the Bafforr branches and now held her near its own trunk, a meter or two above the ground. Every time she struggled, the vesuvague squeezed a little tighter.

Either it would crush her, or it would keep squeezing until she couldn't move. Then it would wait for her to die of thirst.

She gave one final struggle. The tree fought back, wrapping a thin vine around her face. Her mouth was covered. It was getting hard to breathe, and her vision started to blur. Soon another vine would cover her eyes, and she'd be blind and helpless.

At least, she thought, *I won't be caught by Spore.*

Just before the last vine fell into place, she saw a

figure walk toward her. Through her bleary eyes, she could just make out the hammerheaded silhouette of an Ithorian. It reached out to touch her.

Everything went black.

Tash opened her eyes with a start.

Strong but gentle hands held her down, and a soothing voice said, "You are safe."

Tash blinked to clear her eyes. She was lying in a large cave. A small campfire crackled nearby. Over it, someone had placed a simple grill and a stone bowl full of bubbling liquid. The smoke from the fire rose up, mixing with the scent of the liquid to fill the cave with a pleasant odor.

Tash sat up slowly and realized she was sitting next to Fandomar. Relief, warmer than the fire, flooded through her. "I'm glad you're all right!"

Fandomar nodded. "The feeling in my legs returned soon after you left. I guessed where you were going, and I knew the danger, so I decided not to wait for you."

"How did you find me?" Tash asked.

Fandomar handed her a cup of the steaming liquid. It tasted like vegetables. "The Bafforr trees told me," she said simply. "After I found you, I brought you here."

Fandomar's hand swept across the cave. The darkness was lit only by fire. In the gloom, Tash saw Ithorians moving about. Most wore simple clothes, or no clothes at all.

"This is the home for some of those who've felt the call of the Mother Forest," Fandomar explained. "As a High Priest, my husband knew they were here, and so did I. This was the only place I could think of."

"We're safe then?" Tash asked.

"For the moment," Fandomar said. "Those who hear the call of the Mother Forest are shy and avoid contact with strangers. They are uncomfortable being near us even now, and permit it only because my husband was a High Priest. They will avoid anyone else they see, and so they are not likely to be captured by Spore." Fandomar's eyes darkened. "But Spore must be stopped. Eventually, it will absorb every being on this planet. No place will be safe."

Tash thought of Hoole and Zak. "What is Spore?"

Fandomar sighed, then began, "The story is sad, both for my people and for me. We Ithorians are more than just gardeners. We have learned to create new forms of plant life by splicing the genes of one plant with those of another. Usually, we do this to make stronger, healthier versions of a plant."

"Using DNA," Tash said.

"Exactly." Fandomar continued, "About four hundred years ago, my people took their experiments too far. Using the genes of the vesuvague tree and the Bafforrs, along with some other things, they created a new form of life. Like the vesuvague, this creation snared its victims in its tentaclelike vines. It also had a group mind like the Bafforr trees. However, unlike the wise Bafforrs, its mind was evil.''

"Why?" Tash asked.

Fandomar raised her hands in that shruglike motion. "Who can say? Perhaps it was driven mad by the process that created it. I don't know. But whatever the reason, a change occurred. The Bafforrs have a peaceful desire to let their collective mind grow. In Spore, this desire became a hunger. Spore exists to snare the minds of everyone it meets and bring them under its control.''

"How many beings," Tash said, almost afraid to ask, "could Spore control?"

"Thousands," Fandomar replied in the gloom. "Maybe millions.''

Tash's heart skipped a beat. She imagined whole worlds under the control of Spore's dark tentacles. When she spoke, her voice shook. "How did the Ithorians stop it?"

"With luck," Fandomar replied. "And the help of the Jedi. There were still Jedi Knights four hundred years ago. Even so, it wasn't easy. It took almost a hundred years to rid Ithor of the Spore creature."

"Do you know how they did it?"

"No. There were records, but they were erased by the Empire.''

Tash nodded grimly. That made sense. When the Emperor took power, he had hunted down and killed the Jedi Knights. Then he had erased almost every reference to the Jedi Knights from libraries across the galaxy.

By wiping out the record of the Jedi work on Ithor, the Empire might have erased the means of stopping Spore.

"I do know this," Fandomar said. "Spore was sealed up in the asteroid tomb for a reason. In the vacuum of space, it becomes dormant and powerless."

"Why didn't they just kill it?" Tash asked.

Fandomar frowned. "The Law of Life applies to all creatures. We created Spore. Did that give us a right to kill it? Besides, my people thought the solution would work. Spore was helpless in the asteroid tomb. It must have an oxygen atmosphere and a host to occupy."

"You mean like Hodge," Tash said. She guessed the rest. "Hodge and his men thought there was treasure down there. They wanted to keep it for themselves. When Jerec arrived, Hodge must have thought his only chance was to stall the Imperials and raid the tomb himself. He must have made up the story about the space slugs' feeding time, and then he and one of his men opened the tomb."

Fandomar nodded. "In its dormant form, Spore would have looked like a small hard shell, maybe even a valuable stone. Somehow, Spore awakened and was able to infect Hodge before he left the tomb.''

"But why did Hodge kill his partner?'' Tash asked. "Why not just infect him?''

"They were still in space,'' Fandomar explained. "Spore cannot infect people across the vacuum of space. Hodge undoubtedly put the Spore creature near his own skin, but once Spore had infected him, it could not get at the other miner. I think that the other miner saw Hodge being infected. Since Spore couldn't reach out with its tentacles to control the other miner, it used Hodge's body and a vibroblade to kill the miner and keep him quiet.''

Tash's eyes lit up. "And you were the one who blew up the mining station.''

Fandomar nodded. "I had to stop Spore, but I didn't know at the time who was infected. I couldn't allow the creature into an oxygen atmosphere, so I destroyed the station's controls. Then I lied about the environmental controls aboard my ship to make sure everyone kept their spacesuits on. It bought me some time.''

The heavy tone in Fandomar's voice caught Tash's attention. "Why have you gotten so involved in this?''

"Because,'' Fandomar said, "it is all my fault!''

CHAPTER 17

"What do you mean it's your fault?" Tash asked.

The shadows of the cave seemed to wrap around Fandomar as she answered. "The Ithorians have kept Spore a secret for four hundred years. We knew that someone might be tempted to open the tomb. Only the High Priests knew of the tomb's location."

Fandomar sighed, then continued. "I learned about its location accidentally, from my husband, who was a High Priest. The Imperial officer who forced my husband to reveal his secrets was a terrible, violent man. He would have killed my husband and wiped out an entire forest of Bafforr trees without thinking. I was afraid he would not be satisfied with the secrets my husband gave him"—Fandomar shuddered—"so I told him about Spore!"

Tash gently put her hand over Fandomar's. She had guessed the rest. "You said you volunteered to make the shuttle run to the mining station. Was that so you could keep an eye on the tomb?"

Fandomar nodded. "I had to make sure no one opened it, especially after the miners discovered the slug hole. I thought I could manage, until the Imperials arrived."

Tash wondered how Jerec had learned about Spore. She shrugged. The Empire was evil and corrupt. Officers traded information to get more power. Jerec had probably bought or stolen the secret of Spore from someone, then kept it for himself. It didn't matter.

Tash had more important things to worry about. She stood up. She had been sipping Fandomar's broth as they talked, and she felt better. Fandomar followed her as they walked toward the front of the cave. The planet-dwelling Ithorians shied away as they passed.

"Fandomar, isn't there any way to stop Spore and save the others? Or at least to warn the herd ships?"

The Ithorian shook her head. "There are no communication devices here," she said, pointing out the primitive lifestyle of the Ithorians around them. "As for stopping Spore, I have a theory. Hodge is the first person infected. That makes him the primary host, or the main body. If he is forced into space, I think Spore will go dormant and lose his power over the others."

They reached the front of the cave. They were on a

mountainside. Below them, the Ithorian forest stretched on forever. It was an inspiring view, but Tash's shoulders slumped. "We might as well just wish it away. I doubt Hodge will accidentally step out of an airlock."

Fandomar agreed. "There is only one thing in our favor at the moment. When Spore and his victims were looking for you, I sabotaged the medical craft with this." She held up a blaster. "I found it near the wreckage of the cargo ship."

Tash guessed that it was probably the same blaster Hoole had been holding just before the cargo ship started its fall.

"I am unfamiliar with weapons," Fandomar admitted, "but I set it on its highest strength and fired into the ship's engines. They will not function. Since no other Ithorians come down here, Spore will be unable to find any more victims. He still controls the crew of the medical shuttle, your brother, and your uncle, but at least he has been neutralized. There is no way for Spore to leave the surface of the planet now."

But Fandomar spoke too soon. Even as the words left her mouth, an Imperial shuttle streaked over their heads and shot toward the forest floor.

Tash and Fandomar hurried through the forest as quickly and silently as possible. Around them, Tash knew, were half a dozen of the shy, planet-dwelling

Ithorians. But they moved so stealthily that she never saw or heard them.

Fandomar had persuaded the Ithorians to help with a desperate plan. They knew that Spore would try to steal the next ship that came by, Imperial or not. Fandomar's native friends would cause a distraction, then vanish into the forest. Meanwhile, Tash and Fandomar would sneak on board and steal the ship, or at least damage it so that Spore could not fly to a more populated area.

They reached the clearing where the Imperial shuttle had landed, and crept closer. From behind a Bafforr tree, Tash saw that the shuttle's ramp was lowered. At the foot of the ramp stood Jerec himself. Facing him stood Spore, in Hodge's body, with his victims crowding behind him. Zak and Hoole were among them.

Silently, Tash cursed herself for not taking the blaster from Fandomar. She had a clean shot at Spore. But she doubted that killing one of Spore's victims would kill Spore itself. Besides, she had to admit, she wasn't sure she could bring herself to shoot someone in cold blood.

"You were brave to come alone," Spore said in a half dozen voices.

Jerec sneered. "I am not about to feed you any more victims, Spore."

Spore laughed. The sight of her brother and uncle laughing with the others made Tash wince. "So you think you know what I am," said Spore. "Let me give you a closer look!"

Spore and all his servants opened their eyes and mouths. A forest of vinelike tentacles shot toward the dark-cloaked Imperial.

Jerec raised one hand. Tash felt a ripple of dark-side power flow from his fingertips. When Spore's tentacles met the dark-side energy, they withered and died in midair.

Jerec snorted. "Your power is hardly a match for the dark side of the Force." He cast an evil grin at Spore. "However, you have your uses."

"If you are so powerful," Spore said, "what do you want with me?"

Jerec smoothed the band of black cloth that covered his eyes. "Your ability to control thousands of other beings is of use to me. I do not mean to be the Emperor's servant forever. I have plans of my own, and to achieve my plans I need an army. Unfortunately, most Imperial soldiers are loyal to the Emperor himself. I want you to take control of the Imperial army and navy, so that, through you, the soldiers will follow my commands."

"And you become the new Emperor," Spore guessed.

"Exactly," Jerec agreed.

Spore growled. "Why should I help you?"

Jerec smiled. He looked relaxed, but Tash could still feel the dark-side energy pulsing around him like a shield.

"I will give you a ship to take you off this planet."

Spore scoffed. "I will have that anyway, soon enough. Before long all the herd ships will be part of me, and I will use them to spread across the galaxy."

"Tedious work. Slow work," Jerec said. "Imagine how much faster it would be if you had your own Star Destroyer."

Spore seemed intrigued. He listened as Jerec explained. "My Star Destroyer, the *Vengeance,* is orbiting overhead. Its crew obeys my orders, but only because I serve the Emperor. I want them to obey *me,* not the Emperor. Do you understand?"

Spore nodded.

"Enslave them. Guarantee that they will do whatever I ask. Do that, and I will give you whole worlds to conquer. But we must leave immediately."

There was a pause. All of Spore's bodies—Hodge, Zak, Hoole, and the four Ithorians—stood absolutely still while the monster was deep in thought.

Then all the voices said at once, "Agreed."

Fandomar's friends chose that moment for their distraction. A shadowy figure flitted through the edge of the clearing. Then another, and another. Spore started toward them.

"Leave them!" Jerec ordered, following after. "Get aboard the shuttle. There's no time."

"No!" Spore shouted. "They're mine! They will join me."

116

"Remember—the ship! The entire crew! They are yours!" Jerec said.

Spore hesitated for a split second, then divided himself in two. The four captured Ithorians ran into the forest. Hodge, Zak, and Hoole went onto Jerec's shuttle. Spore could control them all, from anywhere.

None of them had noticed, during the distraction, two figures scrambling aboard the empty shuttle.

Tash and Fandomar had barely crammed themselves into a small storage bay in the back of the shuttle before the ship lifted off.

Only after the shuttle had left the planet did Tash have time to consider what in the galaxy she was doing. She had just sneaked on board an Imperial shuttle that carried a master of the dark side of the Force and an evil parasite called Spore.

CHAPTER

18

For several tense minutes, neither Tash nor Fandomar spoke. Tash listened with her ears—and with her mind. She guessed that Jerec was still concentrating on shielding himself from Spore. That, plus the attention required to fly his own ship, should keep the dark-sider from sensing their presence.

As for anyone hearing them, they were back near the thruster ports. The sound of the ship's engines would mask their conversation.

"What now?" Fandomar whispered.

"I have a plan," Tash said, which was half true. "I think we can stop the Star Destroyer and save Zak and Hoole. But it means relying on something I'm not sure I can do. And I need your help."

Fandomar stated firmly, "I cannot break the Law of Life."

Tash tried to smile. "You'll just have to bend it a little."

The shuttle glided quickly toward the massive Star Destroyer orbiting Ithor and slid smoothly into the docking bay. Tash and Fandomar weren't sure what happened next. They could hear very little. But from the few sounds that trickled into their hiding spot, they could guess. Spore had branched out and was infecting everyone in the docking bay. In a matter of minutes, he had spread from a handful of victims to hundreds.

With painfully slow, quiet movements, Tash slipped out of the storage bin and tiptoed toward the front of the shuttle. She crawled on her stomach until she reached the hatch, and peeked outside.

The docking bay of the Star Destroyer was huge. It should have been filled with noise.

This one was quiet as a tomb.

Tash guessed that all the infected crewmen were now moving around the ship, infecting even more Imperials.

Only two figures were left standing alone on the main deck. When she saw them, Tash almost cried tears of joy. It was Zak and Hoole.

Tash had hoped they would be left behind. She remembered that Spore had captured Zak, and nearly captured her, by sending someone familiar to lure them in. She had guessed that Spore would use the same strategy on the crew of the Star Destroyer. Since Hoole and Zak were outsiders, they would only raise suspicion, so Spore had left them behind.

Now all Tash had to do was save them.

Tash walked up to her uncle and brother as calmly as if they were aboard their own ship. They were standing as still as statues, with their backs to the shuttle. Summoning up all the courage she could manage, she said, "Hi, guys."

Zak and Hoole whirled around as one. "Tash," Spore said through their mouths. "I want you to join me. Now."

"Wait!" Tash said. She was speaking with her mouth, but she was focusing with her mind. She reached out with the Force. Once before she had used the Force to reach into someone's mind. If she could do it again . . .

Hoole and Zak opened their mouths and eyes wide to release the deadly spore tendrils. Then they closed them.

"Zak, Uncle Hoole, it's me, Tash," said Tash, still reaching out with the Force. She tried to imagine the connection between them, a power stronger than Spore.

Hoole blinked.

Zak cocked his head in confusion.

Tash could feel the Force flowing back and forth—

from Tash to Hoole, from Zak to Tash. They *were* connected. It was working!

Then Spore seemed to strengthen his hold. Tash felt herself losing them. The Force connection wasn't broken (it could *never* be broken, she realized), but she didn't know how to use it. She didn't have the skill.

Spore, meanwhile, had everything he needed to fight back. The confused look left Zak's face. He and Hoole belonged to Spore once again.

Dark tentacles burst from their eyes. Vines flew from their mouths.

At the last second, Tash imagined the Force rising up around her like a wall. She didn't know if it was the best thing to do. She didn't even know if it was the right thing to do. All she knew was that she loved her brother and her uncle, and to save them she had to defend herself.

The dark vines stopped in midair and fell to the floor in withered strings.

Zak and Hoole froze for a moment. Tash's knees nearly gave out. Using the Force had taken something out of her. She knew she didn't have the strength to defend herself again.

Fortunately, she didn't have to. In the moment Hoole and Zak hesitated, Fandomar rose up behind them. She aimed the blaster she had carried and fired two quick blasts. Hoole and Zak crumpled to the floor.

Fandomar paused for the briefest instant. She bent

121

down to examine her two victims. Tash saw her relax when she confirmed that they were only stunned. She sighed, "Bent, but not broken."

"Spacesuits and Starflies," Tash said. "And hurry. Spore will know everything that's happened here."

As if to confirm her words, intruder alarms sounded throughout the ship.

The Starflies were easy to find—Jerec and his men had used them not long before. A spacesuit that fit Fandomar took a little longer. Most Imperials were humans, and there was almost no need for alien-sized uniforms. Tash checked three lockers before she found one that came close. The Ithorian's hammerhead was nearly crushed against the sides of the oversized helmet. Her wide-set eyes were so jammed that she could hardly see.

"Is that comfortable enough?" Tash asked.

"I will be less comfortable as one of Spore's victims," Fandomar replied.

The alarms had been going off for over a minute. Spore's entire crew of new slaves would be there any second.

Fandomar and Tash frantically slid Zak and Hoole into spacesuits. Tash grabbed a length of cable she'd found in one of the lockers and tied their hands together.

"There's cargo space behind the Starfly seats," she told Fandomar.

At the far end of the docking bay, a door slid open. A

squad of stormtroopers burst in. Their weapons were drawn, but they did not fire.

They belonged to Spore. And they wanted Tash to join them.

"Your uncle will not fit," Fandomar said.

"Make him fit!" Tash screeched. She helped the Ithorian slip the large Shi'ido into the cargo space of Fandomar's vessel, folding his tied hands quickly across his chest.

Tash then jumped into her own Starfly, with Zak's unconscious form crammed in behind her. The stormtroopers were only a dozen yards away. As Tash lifted off in the Starfly, the docking bay's enormous doors started to close. But Spore had moved too slowly. The quick Starflies slipped easily through the opening.

As the two tiny ships darted away from the giant Star Destroyer, Tash heard Fandomar's voice over the intercom. "We can't outrun an Imperial Star Destroyer in these!"

Tash replied, "No, but we can outfly it!"

She pointed her ship toward the asteroid field and hit the accelerator.

CHAPTER 19

Tash banked hard as an asteroid came out of nowhere and nearly crumpled the front end of her Starfly.

She checked her scanner, hoping the *Vengeance* had fallen back.

It had gained.

Spore was following them.

Tash wasn't sure whether Spore would come after them. After all, it had an entire Star Destroyer at its disposal—why chase down a few more victims? She had gambled on something Fandomar had told her, that Spore was driven to infect *every* being it met. The creature itself had confirmed that when it pursued the Ithorians in the forest.

Spore wanted everyone to join it.

As the two Starflies flicked in and out among the

asteroids, the *Vengeance* surged forward. Its pointed front end sliced into the asteroid field like a knife. Power turbolasers blasted any space rocks that came close. The asteroids that weren't destroyed bounced off the Destroyer's deflector shields.

So far, so good, Tash thought. She took a few deep breaths, trying to regain the awareness of the Force she'd had a few minutes before.

"That won't work, you know," Spore whispered in her ear.

Tash nearly jumped out of her skin. Zak was awake. He had spoken through the comlink in his helmet, and hers had picked it up.

Tash tried to calm her racing heart. The Starfly didn't provide any atmosphere of its own, she reminded herself. The inside of the little ship was just like the vacuum of space. Spore couldn't infect her. And since Zak was tied up, he didn't pose much of a threat, either.

"I'm going to warn the Empire," Tash threatened. "You'll be hunted down and destroyed before you can infect one more person."

"You'll never get the chance," Spore said in Zak's voice. Tash was surprised at how *evil* her brother could sound. "You will join me. You'll be a part of me. Didn't you want to become one with the Force? Isn't that what you told me?"

"I told *Zak*!" Tash snapped.

She swerved just in time to avoid another asteroid. Spore was trying to distract her. She couldn't listen.

Spore continued, "The Force is nothing. If it ever existed, it belonged to Jedi who died years ago. I can offer you something more. Join me, and you will join thousands, millions of others." Spore laughed. "You are just what I've been waiting for. Jerec thinks I'm mad for chasing you down, but *I* control the crewmen, so *I* control the ship. He's right here with me, on the bridge of the Star Destroyer."

For an instant, Tash let herself be impressed by Spore's power. He could be in many places at once. He was with Tash in the Starfly, and he was on board the Imperial ship. It was frightening.

Spore continued. "Jerec doesn't know of your Force sensitivity. But I do. Should I tell him?" the creature taunted. "Or should I keep it to myself? You know, you're not strong enough to stop me. Not nearly strong enough. Once you're under my control, I'll make you my primary host. I will be you."

Tash saw what she was looking for. A cluster of moon-sized asteroids spackled with cavernous holes. She aimed for the middle of the cluster.

"You'll have to catch me first," she said through clenched teeth.

Again, Spore laughed. "The asteroid field won't stop me. The *Vengeance* is powerful enough to survive the collisions. The asteroids are nothing."

Tash plunged into the enormous cluster of asteroids, her Starfly buzzing them like a swamp midge darting around a herd of nerfs.

Behind it, the Star Destroyer continued cutting a path, whole batteries of turbolasers firing at once. Dozens of asteroids were blasted into space dust.

Waves of rubble showered the large asteroids, causing vibrations in the rock.

Inside the asteroids, creatures stirred.

The Star Destroyer entered the cluster.

Spore grinned. "I have you now."

Tash felt a tractor beam lock onto her tiny Starfly. The ship froze instantly in place. She was caught.

At the same time, something huge and gray launched itself like a missile from a cavern. The space slug had never before encountered anything its own size, and it lunged forward eagerly.

The giant worm struck, battering the *Vengeance* before it bounced off the Star Destroyer's shields.

"You see?" Spore said through Zak's mouth. "My ship can withstand—"

Zak's mouth stopped working.

Another space slug had attacked from another angle. The Star Destroyer shook.

"You were saying?" Tash said.

The tractor beam dropped off. Tash hit the accelerator and slipped out of the asteroid cluster.

Behind her, the *Vengeance* tried to change course, but

it was attacked again and again. The two space slugs were too stubborn, or too stupid, to give up. And Tash doubted that Spore knew how to command the Star Destroyer. It moved sluggishly, slowly. The ship had been hit a dozen times before it managed to turn around.

By that time, its shields were failing, and with its shields gone, the Star Destroyer could not fend off the asteroids. And at nearly two kilometers long, it was a big target. Space rocks slammed into its hull at a hundred different points. Plumes of fire started lifting from its main deck. A moment later, the bridge exploded.

Tash saw a gaping hole open up the side of the starship. As she reached the edge of the asteroid field, she imagined the vacuum of space rushing in to find Spore.

EPILOGUE

"So I have an evil laugh, huh?" Zak asked. He gave a wicked-sounding chuckle.

"Not even close," Tash replied.

They were aboard the *Tafanda Bay,* lounging in one of the floating city's many parks. All of them seemed relieved except Fandomar, who sat with her eyes downcast and muttering to herself in sorrowful tones.

Her theory had been correct. When the hole had opened up in the side of the Star Destroyer, the air inside had escaped, just as it had at the mining facility. Spore and his minions had been unable to seal the damage, and soon the entire ship had been exposed to airless space.

Spore had been neutralized.

Soon after the *Vengeance* had lost power and started drifting, Zak had fainted. When he came to his senses a few hours later, he had no memory of the time of his infection. Neither he nor Hoole had asked for details, which was fine with Tash. She still turned pale at the thought of the weird tentacles hurtling from their mouths and eyes. She didn't need to describe it.

Hoole walked up to them. "The *Shroud* is refueled," their uncle said. "It's time to go."

Tash put her hand on Fandomar's shoulder. "Will you be all right?"

Fandomar sighed. "I do not know. I have committed

a crime far worse than my husband's," she said. "He gave up our secret technology to save the Bafforr trees. I betrayed the Law of Life and helped destroy all those people on the Star Destroyer."

"But you probably saved countless lives by doing so," Hoole replied.

"Besides," Tash argued, "*you* didn't do anything to those Imperials. You were only following me."

Fandomar blinked. "I'm afraid my conscience may not be as forgiving as you are."

Tash got to her feet. "Please don't feel bad, Fandomar. You're a hero. I mean, Spore is dead, right?" she asked. "If Zak and Uncle Hoole and those four Ithorians have all returned to normal, Spore must have died."

Fandomar nodded. "I hope so."

On the outskirts of the asteroid field, Imperial salvage crews sorted through the wreckage of the *Vengeance* that floated around in space. There wasn't much left to pick up, but they'd been ordered to scan the garbage with extra-fine sensors. The order had come from Jerec himself, who had survived the wreck by escaping aboard a Starfly moments before destruction.

The salvage crews grumbled, and swept the asteroid field again. Hardly anything showed up on their scopes.

So far, a few small objects had escaped their attention. If they kept looking they might find, drifting in the debris, a few undamaged TIE fighters, the ship's computer core with all its Imperial secrets intact, and, nearby, a human body and a dark object the size of a human fist. It looked like a large seed.

The corpse was nothing important—just the body of someone named Hodge, who had once been chief partner of a mining station. He had died when the Star Destroyer lost its air.

Beside it, the small fist-sized object floated.

And waited. Eventually, someone would find it. Someone would pick it up . . .

Hoole, Tash, and Zak continue their journeys to the darkest reaches of the galaxy in *The Doomsday Ship,* the next book in the Star Wars: Galaxy of Fear series. For a sneak preview, turn the page!

AN EXCERPT FROM

BOOK 10

THE DOOMSDAY SHIP

A moment later, Zak found himself looking at a computer-generated image of deep space. Slowly, a small ship appeared. It was an Imperial TIE fighter that appeared to have been damaged.

"Is this a combat game?" Zak asked. "What am I supposed to do?"

There was a small box at the bottom of the screen, and in it words appeared. YOU'RE AN IMPERIAL TIE FIGHTER PILOT. YOUR SHIP HAS BEEN DAMAGED AND YOU NEED TO REGAIN POWER BEFORE REBEL FORCES ARRIVE.

Zak frowned. He didn't like playing an Imperial. But a game was a game.

YOU NEED TO FIND THE ACCESS CODE THAT

WILL REPAIR YOUR SHIP. BUT YOU MUST DO IT BEFORE THE ENEMY ARRIVES!

Next to the TIE fighter, a series of codes appeared. The frown remained on Zak's face. This wasn't a very exciting game. Sighing, he picked one code and typed it in. It didn't work. A little more interested, he typed in another, and another, until finally, one of them worked. A new line of text appeared on the screen: FIRST LEVEL SAFEGUARDS DISENGAGED.

"Prime," Zak said to himself. Then he typed, "Okay, what now?"

No answer.

"SIM?" Zak typed.

ZAK. THERE SEEMS TO BE A SLIGHT PROBLEM ELSEWHERE ON THE SHIP. I NEED TO DEVOTE ALL BANKS TO IT. EXCUSE ME.

The computer screen blinked and went dark.

"What a great computer," Zak said to no one in particular. He stood up and went outside, where Tash and Dash Rendar were still talking.

"Tash, the strangest thing just happened," Zak said. "I was just on the computer, and it started talking to me."

"Most computers talk more than is good for them," Dash said.

"Not like this," Zak replied. "This one is more like a living being than anything I've ever seen, even a droid. It's called SIM."

Dash's eyes widened. "SIM? What kind of name is that?"

Zak's answer was drowned out by a sudden blast of noise. Alarm bells rang, filling the hallways with ear-piercing shrieks. All three humans clamped their hands over their ears, but the sound reached right through and stabbed into their brains.

Louder even than the alarm bells, a computerized voice boomed over the ship's loudspeakers:

"Evacuate ship! This is not a drill. Evacuate ship!"

Journey to a galaxy far, far away with these other
exciting **STAR WARS** books

Shadows of the Empire
A Junior Novelization by Christopher Golden, Based
on the *New York Times* Bestseller

And read more about the Star Wars heroes
in new stories that take up where
Return of the Jedi left off:

#1 *The Glove of Darth Vader*
#2 *The Lost City of the Jedi*
#3 *Zorba the Hutt's Revenge*
#4 *Mission from Mount Yoda*
#5 *Queen of the Empire*
#6 *Prophets of the Dark Side*

ABOUT THE AUTHOR

John Whitman has written several interactive adventures for *Where in the World Is Carmen Sandiego?,* as well as many Star Wars stories for audio and print. He is an executive editor for Time Warner AudioBooks and lives in Encino, California.